Something New

By

Kemka Ezinwo

D1714002

Mary-Immanuella and Benjamin

Mrs Louisa Iquo Ezinwo

Late Sir and Lady P. E. B. Inyang

Peter Onyekabu, Temitope Fadeyi, Chukwuemeka Eze, Enoima Abraham, Inebi Douglas, Usman Dhalhatu, Ucho Ndumele, Jason Dewkurun, Khotobar David, Mrs. Damole, Evelyn Arthur, Grace Abimbola, Abimbola Makanjuola and Pastor Efe Oluwatosin

One

Athena couldn't quite disguise her eagerness to see Desmond, her high school crush. With smoky eyes like Kate Moss' she spiralled down the stairs to meet him.

Desmond appraised her; she wore a cobalt-blue polo shirt by *Abercrombie*, ruffle mini-skirt paired with bright pink skate shoes. His expression moved from surprise to disgust to concern in less than a minute, but she was too excited to notice. "Wow, you're all dressed up though!"

"I know right?" Athena grinned sheepishly.

He looked at her blankly.

"Well...I'm ready where are we going? You never said –"

"Sorry, I'm a bit lost here. Were we going somewhere?"

Athena was now the one wearing a blank stare, which gradually turned into a look of confusion.

"Well, if you dressed up for me, then you've wasted your time. I wasn't asking for a date."

"But..."

"But what?"

"Des–"

"It was a dare, all right? A dare! I can't go on a date with you!" He hissed.

"Wh-what?"

"I couldn't risk tossing £5000 to any of my friends, nor would you in my position?" he asked matter-of-factly.

Athena's world started spinning; she staggered back and forth trying to regain her balance.

"Excuse me." He pressed the buzzer to let himself out.

She sat on one of the stairs, and watched him walk away. She shut her eyes, trying to block, or possibly erase what had just happened. Her inhaler was out of reach so she tried to steady her breath. A few minutes later, a call came through her *Nokia 6600*. She ignored it.

She only checked her phone when the ringtone she had set for messages from Nadine came on.

She read it quickly, and her heart hit the floor; she was going to be the new buzz on campus. Brenda Swanson, the president of Communication Society, advised her to stay off campus for a few weeks, or until there was another sensational news for the university magazine – the girl was paying a debt she owed Athena for helping her prepare for an exam.

As the reality of the event began to sink in, she started to tug her hair, oblivious to the pain from the hairpins piercing her skin. The cool spring wind sweeping through the window did nothing to dissipate her anger. She didn't realise she had been crying until she tasted salt. She ignored everyone who asked her if she was all right while they were climbing the stairs. Others gave varied looks from pity and sympathy to irritation and anger. She clasped her hand over her mouth and sobbed aloud.

Exhausted, she wiped her eyes and looked down. She saw a rubber band. She yawned, picked it up, and used it to pull her hair into a pony tail then yawned again. She rested her chin on the ball of her palm, then glanced at the door and sighed; the murkiness of the night sky outside was how she felt inside. A student came in, and put a wedge to prop the door - *he probably lost his keys*. She felt a sudden pang when she heard laughter nearby and curled up into a ball. Gradually she calmed down when she realised it was coming from some drunken student party.

She must have been there a long time because it became very quiet. Irritated at her irregular breathing, she tried to steady her breath. She opened her palms and saw they were red. Frowning, she smelled her hands; they were bleeding. Expressionless, she stared at it for a while, then wiped her hand on her skirt as she made a personal declaration: she wasn't only going to get a first class, she was going to be the best student, then she was going to frustrate Desmond Stones emotionally and ruin his chances of graduating with a first class - she knew he was pilfering the question papers.

She got up slowly, and started climbing the stairs when she heard Nadine's voice.

"Ol'girl o! Guess who I saw at that restaurant em...Venezia Italian, this morning?"

Andrew, of course.

"Guess nawh!"

Athena gave a nonchalant look, and shrugged.

"Desmond," Nadine said, drooling.

"Okay," Athena retorted, suddenly overcome with weariness.

"What's up? I thought you'd be glad."

Athena gave her a wry smile.

"Hey! Wetin hapun? Sorry, what happened? You're dressed up and gloomy. So that stupid girl didn't make your hair again. Come, let's go and collect the money back. I knew we should have gone to the salon. I'm so sorry. Come nawh!" Nadine knew something was wrong when she tried to grab Athena's hand, and Athena had shrunk back. "Wetin hapun? What is it?" she asked with concern.

"Nothing."

"Nothing? You expect me to swallow that *abi*?" Nadine chortled.

"Nothing," Athena confirmed in irritation. Before Nadine could respond she added, "Please don't ask, and leave it at that."

"Hhm." Nadine sighed thoughtfully and they climbed the stairs to their floor in silence.

Athena never told Nadine what happened that night, and with time Nadine's eagerness to know waned.

3

♥♥♥

Temitope loved the winter season only when she was stuck in the house. She grumbled nonstop, trudging through the snow, from the make shift car park to the reception to find out the venue for the PTA meeting. She was late again. The other women's eyes were stuck on her like bees chasing an intruder, and it didn't help that her shoes squeaked. She had gotten thick skinned after their constant badgering of the head teacher for accepting two more black children against their quota of non-white British intakes.

Unlike Temitope, who sometimes came off as rude for her brute bluntness, they cowered behind each other. They couldn't outwardly condemn the head teacher because it would imply that they were racist. The Head teacher of the all girls' school was no different; she just needed money to keep the school up and running.

Temitope's mind drifted back to a few years ago when her daughters were first introduced to the English education. It was unusual to admit more than one coloured child per unit of ten pupils. She saw the opportunity when she discovered that the school was impecunious. After much beguiling Olamide succumbed to the wishes of his wife. The Head Teacher, Mrs. Olsen, the all prim and proper American, didn't take kindly to it, but she didn't have a choice. One day, Temitope stumbled upon an advert, at a groceries store and saw the opportunity as an escape from boredom. She became the nanny to an autistic child, named David who happened to be the Head Teacher's child.

It was a cold, rainy spring day and everyone remained inside despite the fact the PTA meeting had ended thirty minutes earlier.

The Head Teacher's 'associates' - better known by other parents as the 'gossip committee' – were huddled in a corner, arguing in hushed tones. The 'associates' were pioneer members of the school's board which included Portia. Portia was daughter of a former Mayor of Birmingham, whose curiosity knew no bounds, and whose tongue was as elite and ferocious as a boomslang.

Temitope wore a mischievous smile, gleefully rubbed her palms together and walked to the group. Then she 'accidentally' dropped a picture in their midst, making it a curious part of their discussion. Mrs. Olsen, the mockingly rich, ugly and holier than thou dame, had a child out of wedlock? A child not even her husband knew of. Mrs. Olsen turned as red as strawberry, when it got to be her turn to hold the picture. Temitope had to admit the little boy was rather handsome and more than genius for his age.

Temitope noticed Mrs. Olsen retreating and went to stand behind her, causing Mrs Olsen to bump into her. The woman gave her a wry smile, but Temitope never missed an opportunity, so she cashed in on it; her children would be staying on.

♥♥♥

Olamide was almost sure he was roasting like the goat used for thanksgiving lunch two months ago to celebrate the new millennium. He slackened the knot of his tie.

His mouth was dry and saliva seemed scarce - he had already downed close to two litres of water. He didn't have the courage to remove his jacket, because he wasn't wearing a singlet under his *Pierre Cardin* Shirt.

He felt an uncomfortable sensation crawl down his spine, his handkerchief was already sodden. Then, the cloudless blue was suddenly covered in fluffy grey and it began to rain. By the time they got to where the containers were, the parched ground was sopping. He looked down but couldn't find his feet; his blue trousers were now red and clogged with mud and his handmade Italian shoes had lost the allure. He grumbled.

When they arrived at the container he was supposed to clear, there was no one to meet him. Bored of waiting after only two minutes, he walked down to a customs officer who seemed to be doing some checks. Olamide, rather curious, beckoned the officer who reluctantly came towards him. He asked the officer questions and when he was not forthcoming with answers Olamide brought out a wad of ₦1, 000 notes.

The officer licked his lips and a second after money had exchanged hands, information started rolling out of his tongue like waterfall. At the end of the leak, the officer frowned and moved his mouth though no words came out, then squinted with one eye and shrugged before removing the money from his pocket and tucking it into his battered shoes.

The news unsettled Olamide - the containers in question were owned by a prominent businessman with whom he had entered a contract involving all his savings and more. The man was now under investigation. From what he got they were reliably informed that he had contraband which they were sure included hard drugs. Olamide asked about wiggling out of it, but the reply was that the man was to be used as scapegoat - to serve as a deterrent to further abusers. The walk to his car felt endless: he knew his feet touch the ground but felt like he was in someone else's body.

"Oga, your wife called you, Sir." Olamide's driver muttered as he climbed down to opened the car door for his boss.

He didn't respond.

The driver repeated the question and shrugged when he got no response.

Olamide walked into the car slowly like a woman nearing her time. He sat at the edge the chair, his knees locked together as he tried to hug himself while staring blankly at the back of the passenger seat. He didn't take notice of the door being shut or the rest of the journey home. His driver knew something was wrong when the man who usually cracked sultry jokes about any woman they passed, looked out of the window through the tinted glass with solemnly.

When he got home, he practically dragged his limbs up the stairs. Stella, the housekeeper handed him a letter marked 'urgent'. He refused to accept it because he knew it was from the bank: his loan was already two weeks overdue. The landline started to ring. Stella answered the call and quickly brought the cordless phone to him with outstretched arms, "It's your wife Sir."

"Tell her I can't talk to her right now," he said in an uneven tone.

"Sir, I have never seen you like this," she said and trailed after him until they got to his room. He entered his room before she could say anything else and shut the door behind him. She was tempted to go in after him, but she heard the lock turn. Stella stomped her feet in frustration, which was infused with irritation and further infuriated by his wife's phone call. She was the only who called his *Econet* number at that time of the day. She stared at the phone, sulking and with undisguised displeasure. She had spent most of the day in the salon and he didn't notice.

♥♥♥

Moses tipped the ginger beer bottle and tapped it on the glass to catch the last few drops while he flicked the pen in his other hand. He wondered why he decided to go on to do his Masters when his friends went back to Nigeria after their first degree, except those whose parents were wealthy. Bored with studying, he decided to browse the internet. He had received a message from a friend.

He double clicked the title. When he tried to refresh the page, it went off completely. He was curious to know if the 'Ola Wizzy' he saw was the same person he knew back in his university days back home. Sighing, he checked his wallet hopefully, and retrieved only one penny.

The phone began to ring, but he ignored it until the third

ring. He picked it up, pretending to be someone else and was relieved when he found out it was just a marketer. He barely replaced the receiver when someone knocked on his door.

He yanked it open. Irritated he asked, "Hello! How may I help you?"

"Chill out okay? I have a letter for you," she said, dancing on the same spot like someone who desperately needed to use the toilet, but it was to emphasize her large breasts.

Moses arched his brow, trying not to look down at them.

She eyed him and said, "Someone must have mistaken my room for yours."

Mh-huh! Because we're bearing the same name abi? "I see!" Moses said. He nodded slowly and squinted. Then he leaned on the door post, cocked his head and folded his arms in front of him as he waited for her next move. He knew she had been intercepting his letters. She wore a red tube blouse that barely covered her breasts and a black micro mini leather skirt, but he wasn't interested in her, not when he had an eye for the lady in the flat next to hers.

"This came for you," she said.

"Thank you!" He smiled sweetly.

"I..." She cleared her throat. "I'm organising a small dinner today for close friends and, well, some have called... and well... I was hoping you'll come and -"

"I'll think about it."

Well think fast! She smiled unrepentantly, waiting for an idea to pop into her head then she reluctantly slinked back to her flat.

He watched her open the door to her room and disappears. He didn't want any relationship that would require maintenance and was even more interested in the flat after hers. Every man in the building had a keen interest in winning her affection. She had all of the features of a plus-size super model, independent and most importantly, rich. She moved in there three months ago.

He only got to know her as Cora last week when he went

into the Tesco. He saw her first, but feigned ignorance of her presence until she smiled at him. He smiled back and busied himself with the label on the ginger beer bottle as she waltzed pass him dispersing a sweet fragrance.

He turned slightly and saw her sweep a few strands of hair behind her ear. He walked slowly to the till but she was already there disposing of all of the copper coins from her burnt orange purse to a tin for a charity. He was surprised at how angry he was that the copper coins were not being handed to him.

He pulled the curtain open so hard it fell, and when he couldn't find the brackets to replace it, he wrapped it up and tossed it to the foot of his bed. As he opened the window the smell of food from the Indian takeaway downstairs assaulted him, making his stomach rumble in recognition. It was frustrating to sniff the delightful smell of curry nonetheless he couldn't help sniffing some more. When he couldn't take the torture anymore he rifled through the things Kelechi had left behind for him. He had finished his foodstuff and was glad when he saw two tins of tuna and half a packet of spaghetti.

He looked around his room as he got up. He thrust his hands in the back pockets of his now undersized track suit bottoms. He tucked his dirty clothes into a knapsack and hurried to Kelechi's apartment – she still had two months tenure. She had packed everything except for the electric iron, kettle, washing machine and fridge which he frequently used. She was supposed to give him money to help her move them to storage, but his account was overdrawn. She still sent the money after he had warned her. The clincher was that he also needed to move some of his things at the same time.

He came back to his room, while his clothes were in the washing machine at Kelechi's apartment.

He felt stupid when he noticed that the scantily clad room was like a dump, and to make matters worse, he had a rat's nest under his bed. An hour later he finished packing the rubbish into the bin bag, he was carrying the last set when he found a letter near the door. He scowled as he picked it up, then stretched his hand to drop the letter on the reading desk.

Taking the remaining dirty clothes, he went back to his friend's flat to take his shower; the heating in his house had been cut off. While he was drying himself, he saw Cora cross the road. He quickly put on a set of laundered clothes, not realising that the apple green t-shirt now had blue patchworks. He struggled to adjust the jeans because there were uncomfortable between his thighs while packing the rest of his clothes, then dashed out, heading for his room. He took off his shirt as soon as he entered his room, hating the fact that he couldn't even afford an ordinary fan.

He looked out again. She was coming out of a delicatessen in an adjacent building. He watched her stop to drop something in the bin. Her silvery blonde hair glistened in the imposing sun.

Someone whistled. It was coming from the window opposite Kelechi's own. A red-haired boy was ogling him. He glared at the boy and went back to tidying his laundry then ironed shirts. He was hanging the final piece of cloth in the wardrobe when he heard a rapid knock. The door opened before he signalled anyone in.

"Hi!" Cora said, slowly.

"H-hi!" he stuttered.

"I'm sorry to come in like this, but..."

He ushered her in. She waited for him to shut the door and trotted alongside him. He pulled out the chair by the reading desk for her and sat on the edge of his bed with his hands in his pocket so she couldn't see them shaking. She started rubbing her palm and clasped her hands together in front of her, and said, "I'm not used to this, but I need your help..."

Moses opened his mouth and closed it.

"I..." she cleared her throat. She took two steps towards the bed before sitting beside him.

Moses' heart skipped a beat and increased rhythm.

"You see...." she purred, and gliding her fingers lightly down his arm. He stiffened, not sure which path to take even though fighting was not an option in his mind. One look at her and all his resistance melted.

He lowered his head to give her a kiss and her phone rang. He had never seen an expensive phone so up close and personal. He smooched her and continued to kiss her until she blurted into her phone, "Because you're my husband doesn't mean you have the right to order me around. Fine. I'll be there."

All of the excitement died. Moses swallowed quickly and choked: husband!

Two

Anytime Moses thought of what he had lost and what he was about to lose, his heart raced. He had used his mother's company as lien to secure the loan: a third one. They may be right about a fool at forty, after all that's how old he'll be in a few months. In less than two weeks their external auditors would make their sojourn in Lagos and no excuse will be satiable.

It was a dicey period in the country with every legal entity trying to make their mark. He looked around the room gloomily, as the thought of losing everything conjured up in his mind again. He was going to be late on the mortgage. There was no money in his account. He couldn't tell his wife that the house she lived in with the kids in London was under a mortgage.

The only freehold was the *Ferrari Enzo* he bought for his wife, his mother's *Range Rover P38A*. He smiled as his eyes fell on his limited edition *Porsche 993 911 Turbo S* and *Maserati 3200 GT coupe.* He loved the turbocharged V8 of the *Maserati* because he believed it gave an upward thrust to his boisterous personality.

He was not going to part with those cars, come what may, but he could risk parting with the one he bought Temitope for a good price because she didn't know he had bought her a car. His wife was his number one concern though; he didn't know how to break the news to her, especially over the phone. If he found a way to confide in his wife, then she would stand in for him when his mother came to collect.

He remembered the day his mother gave him the documents after a lot of arm twisting. *Maybe I should have let go. Which of these women is the lesser of two evils? My mother? My wife?* He needed to change his situation and time was running out. D. E. Fubara's advice to join the bunkering business clawed its way back into his thoughts.

He sniggered at the thought because Duncan had an idea of every quick-money making scheme that ever existed; Duncan was his first cousin who had been in Prison in almost every country he visited. The only country he hadn't been incarcerated in was Brazil, where he had a wife and two kids.

Olamide was always immune to these advances, but this time was different. After two hours of restlessness, he dozed off, each time waking up and murmuring: "bunkering".

♥♥♥

Athena hated these Parents Teacher Meetings; everyone seemed to know what was best for the school, yet none of them was willing to go the distance or even lift a pin to save it. The meetings she has had to attend these past weeks had given her more headache than solution so much so, that she had to ask herself if it was worth it. The answer made her smile – although she always came off as weird and unenthusiastic, she did always twist her tongue. *Who's laughing now?*

There was a clamour of indistinguishable voices, followed by hushed talks like a babbling stream. Then a woman towered over her. She looked up to see an oval face with deep set eyes and a broad nose looking at her, and reclined further into her seat to make way for the woman to pass. The woman almost caught Athena staring at her. Athena drank the smell of *Thierry Mugler's Comet*, which engulfed her and reminded her that she needed to get a perfume for her graduation dinner.

The woman gave Athena a querying look.

Athena wilted; blushing almost immediately, from face to neck then shook her head.

The woman looked at her from head to toe, tightened her lips, adjusted herself in her seat to straighten her back, crossed her arms, and smiled a greeting to Mrs. Olsen with a slight nod. Mrs. Olsen gave the woman a despairing look and a placid smile.

Athena decided to keep herself to herself the rest of the evening, which meant she couldn't conduct the survey or any interview.

When the meeting ended, Mrs. Olsen asked to speak to Mrs. Ademinokan. Temitope followed the Head teacher and they walked out briskly. The other women, except a trio at the back of the hall close to the toilet, had formed a band at the buffet table, all oblivious to the Head Teacher's rapid departure. Some were busy stuffing food in their bags, that didn't surprise Athena. What did surprise her was the woman who stuffed an already unscrewed bottle of champagne into her bag. She then saw it as an opportunity to do the survey that the Head teacher blatantly forgot to put on display.

By the time she finished, it was almost ten. She decided to beat traffic by taking the train, cutting across the school lawn and over the three feet barricade to the train station which would take her four minutes rather than fifteen minutes. She saw Mrs. Ademinokan in the car park; her white brocade illuminated in the unlit area of the park. Athena was glad to talk to the woman now that the alcohol still had some effect on her. She had just made a turn beside a four wheel drive when she recognized Mrs. Olsen's voice; the argument was about someone called David.

The argument died down a few minutes later, but Mrs. Olsen blocked Temitope's path and pleaded with her simultaneously but Temitope shoved her as she brushed past her, and started walking in Athena's direction. Athena ducked beside the four wheel drive. Her heart almost stopped beating when the engine of the car beside revved. As the car jerked backwards, Athena hid beside the large dustbin, and waited until the car had sped away.

♥♥♥

Moses took a peek through the peep hole of his door to see Cora opposite him. He hissed, and walked back to what he was doing on his bureau: playing ludo. He sighed each time she knocked, trying to ignore Cora's rapid taps. He didn't have a girlfriend; hadn't had one in just over two years.
He knew that the minute he opened the door, there would be nothing holding him back. He was sure she was intentionally tormenting him. His dilapidated second hand laptop was on. If she wasn't there, he would have been able to go to Kelechi's room to use the internet, even if it meant crouching on toe tips all of the way there.

He was still contemplating when a large brown envelop was slipped under his door. He tore it open quickly, then shrieked away when he saw the letterhead. He remained rooted on the spot, wondering where he was to go from there. He frowned, feeling sure that he didn't owe rent and that he was supposed to have three months remaining. Why would solicitors contact him when he still had over a month's rent – that is if the rent had not been increased without his knowledge? *All those people wen no wan make e better for me God dey see una o!*

♥♥♥

Olamide was glad to hear from Moses, but didn't like his inability to assist him in his predicament.

Time was running out: it had been months now and he hadn't yet told his wife about the loan, the mortgage, or even the collateral, though he was sure she would be secretly glad that his mother's hold over him, i.e. the company, would be history. If only he could tell her that the house she was living in was mortgaged. He had done a lot of running around, achieving nothing, but empty promises and distasteful looks. He couldn't sell anything because he had vowed not to follow in his father's footsteps.

One way or the other Temitope was bound to find out, sooner than later if he didn't sort Stella out. He muttered mournfully as he thought of his wife waking up one night and chopping up his manhood. Each time he tried to buttress the thought by finding a solution that same thought webbed its way through.

He kicked off his shoes, and padded into his walk-in closet. He sat on the stool, then got up abruptly, and tucked his hands into pocket. He looked around him like someone taking one last look before a long journey. He shook his head, and said in a loud voice with outstretched arms, "I sunk everything into you, and I'm the losing party."

His phone started to vibrate. Before he heard the ringtone he knew it was his wife. He picked it up and talked with her for about an hour, never giving anything away. When the call ended, he sighed deeply, relieved and glad that she couldn't see his face.

He glanced up, and sighed again before he started his bedtime routine, starting with emptying his pockets. He sorted the business cards and stopped when he spotted the one from Osagie's brother, looked for Duncan's, and tapped on them a few times before placing them on the dresser.

If I can't get to those dupers, I could get to the rest of the world.

♥♥♥

After reading Kelechi's email, he deleted it, and hissed. He was more concerned with paying his rent than sorting out other people's problems. It's been a year, two months and fourteen days since that letter got to him. His hand started to sweat when he carried it up.

He dropped it on the bed, and rubbed his hands until his palms were warm, then pulled out the letter slowly. He started dancing, jumping. It wasn't for joy and excitement, but out of anger, pain, and a little bit of anguish. *What to do?*

He started pacing around the room, each time increasing speed until he hit the big toe of his right foot at the end of the bed. Two days later he travelled to Birmingham to meet the lawyer. He fell in love with Birmingham; it was a much calmer version of London. The lawyer that wrote him had now retired, and his firm was being run by his only child: Jane Natalie Reginald Portman. She handled the 'leftovers' of her father's clients.

Moses had to admit that the way he hungered for money, he wouldn't have minded having her. He got the sum of £74, 273.42, including interest accumulated five years before he received the letter. He was glad he had opened an account before he sent his passport for the renewal of his visa. *2006 is a good year after all!*

As he came out of Barclay's bank, he saw a law firm for 'people like him' and walked in. He agreed to book an appointment, but scuffed and walked out when he found out it was three weeks from that day. *I'll do it when I get back to London abeg!*

He checked the time and looked at the skies. The weather started to change. He scouted for a shop that sold umbrellas. Not seeing any, he hailed a taxi. He entered every shop he had previously been to with his friends. By the time he came out of the mall, it was already dark. He decided to spend the night in Birmingham.

There were no rooms in the entire hotel. *This is the fourth hotel, for goodness sake!* When he went to Jury's Inn, where he was initially turned down, he pretended to be searching for something and emptied his pockets. At the sight of a wad of £50 notes, a manager appeared. The manager didn't even wait to find out if the money was genuine before telling him that someone had just cancelled.

In a matter of seconds, he was given a key card and ushered into a room on the sixth floor. He felt the lie was stupid when they asked him the type of room he wanted, and listed a number of options. *You didn't have any before.* He had his food in his room after taking his bath. He later found out a major shareholder of Ramadan hotel pretended to be a riffraff and was turned out of the hotel.

After dinner he brought out a notepad and started preparing a strategy for which to go about starting his business. One thing was clear: he wasn't going start a company in London, which meant he would have to relocate to Nigeria. This was a relief since he had no strings to pull him back.

But his resolve changed when he remembered he hadn't been in touch with his home base for almost ten years, then resolved to create a niche for himself, then take his brand to Nigeria. He unpacked his new laptop and smiled, made a call to the reception desk and was given a code to enable him access the internet.

Hours later, he laid out what he was going to wear the following day. Bored with staying indoors and watching the activity of the night life, he got dressed. Looking at the mess he had made on the bed he promised to get a place of his own before Olamide set foot in England. Unknown to him, London was very different from Birmingham.

♥♥♥

Temitope was agitated. She twisted her ring several times, before pulling it off, and tossing it in the sink.

She was tired of Olamide's excuses; she was only human and hadn't felt like a woman in years. She went for a walk, but spent just five minutes outside, it was freezing. She entered her car, and drove for hours before parking in front of a pub. Not thinking, she walked into it, and ordered the most alcoholic drink they had; she later settled for brandy.

It wasn't until she bumped into a bum that she realised she was not tipsy but drunk. She scrambled out of the pub, and staggered to her car. She fumbled with the keys because the keyhole was lopsided; she turned sideways to fix the problem, and landed in the dirt.

"Need help?" Moses asked the woman who almost knocked him out.

Temitope smiled gleefully at him.

He shook his head, tugged the car keys from her clenched fist, and subsequently carried her into her car.

♥♥♥

She woke up, sat up on the couch, and tried to recollect how she got home, all at the same time. She saw snapshots: someone had demanded for her keys; *oh they've stolen the car.* She looked on the table, saw the keys, and frowned. She felt a cold hand on her shoulder, and bolted upright, her head hitting Moses on the face. The water in the glass he held spilled on the royal blue harlequin rug.

Temitope shifted to the opposite end of the sofa, while Moses covered his nose and then stood up holding his nose. She became even more confused, and her mind began to reel. *Oh, did I bring a man home! I brought a man into my house! What if he is was paedophile? Where are my daughters? Oh thank God! Yes, that's right, sleep over. Did he sleep with me? Thank God! Phew, what type of headache is this? If this is how it is, why do people drink?*

Her eyes darted around the room, blinking for a few seconds. Her eyes widened. She stifled a sound when he came close to her: he wore a look of concern. She gulped the water noisily, but declined the tablets he had brought for fear that it may be date-rape drug, even though she could see its name embossed on it.

She started laughing, and held her head in her palms. She still felt light headed. She tried to suppress the urge to puke and choked. He came to her side, and started to massage her back. She leaned into him, not wanting him to stop. She hesitated for a few seconds, and then relaxed.

As something in her stirred, she stiffened then rushed out, covering her mouth and picked up a throw with her free hand. A few minutes later, she came back with another glass, and set it down untouched. She tucked her hand under the throw that was now slung across her shoulder, looked at him long and hard. "Who are you?"

"The man you were in bed with?"

"What? Scratch that o! Wetin?"

"You be naija?"

"Before nkó?"

"Sorry, abeg no vex, wen we enter jand everybody dey form _"

"We no dey jand o!"

"Eh?"

"Jand na USA no be *England*."

"Oh that!"

"Please, please, please, tell me the truth, did something happen?"

He got up. "Why is it important?" he replied and picked up his jacket.

"I was drunk for goodness sake."

"Not that drunk," his said, slinging the jacket over his right hand.

"You want to justify your actions?"

20

"What action is there to justify? My name is Moses, you are -?"

"So nothing happened?" she asked excitedly, and sighed. *Thank God o! Olamide would have killed me!*

"So..."

There was an awkward silence, then the phone rang. Temitope nearly ran to pick it. By the time she hung up, she was sobbing. Olamide's driver's call was to tell her that her maid, Stella, went for an abortion which had turned septic. She was recuperating, but she had refused to mention who was responsible.

"Kai!" she exclaimed and bit her nail. *If it wasn't for his children coming in tomorrow, I'd have left for Nigeria today. What am I doing here anyway? And to imagine that I was feeling sympathetic for that stupid man! Where is that stupid passport sef? I'm going oh! Every time, it has been me that would make all of the sacrifices. Yet what does he do? Nothing Oh! He'd just stay there, and be counting sheep under the skirt of every girl he can get his hands on. Why did I even marry him sef? While I'm here, working my butt off, horny and lonely. Mr. Man is screwing my maid. Why else would she keep it to herself?*

This business that he is using as an excuse to remain in Nigeria will soon end. I'll make sure of it. O God! He didn't even have the decency of wearing condom. O God, I WILL KILL THIS MAN! GOD WILL PUNISH HIM OH! What kind of man did I marry sef? Ah!

She hugged herself, and started sobbing. Unsure of what to do, Moses remained where he was staring at her. She was breathing in short gasps and shaking, her head buried between her knees. Moses sighed, then reluctantly walked to her side. He wrapped his arms around her.

As soon as she stopped crying, she shrugged him off, and asked him to leave. On his way out he spotted some pictures that were knocked down, but one was on the floor, and she was in it with two girls. He smiled, and put it away before walking out.

A few minutes later, she let out a violent scream, then muffled the sound with the maroon coloured throw, and rocked herself.

Moses was back. He pulled her into his arms, and rocked her. It tortured him to be there, but he felt he could overcome his urge.

Temitope curled up beside Moses, and the little restraint he   had,   shut   down   violently.

Three

Olamide had a few contacts in the clearing and forwarding business. Using them, he was able to siphon 3 barrels of crude oil right under the nose of Duncan's friend, a retired Sailor, who had a lot of tentacles in the navy and was greedy. Since the oil was initially bunkered unofficially, they couldn't chase him. All the Sailor had was suspicion and decided to trap Olamide so as to catch him in the act.

In less than two years Olamide had increased it to 8 barrels, so as his friends were recording losses to Pirates, he was recording profits, and was hiking the price. All this time he didn't buy anything. He started laundering his money. Temitope called him several times to ask if he was doing anything illegal - he would deny it – a habit he had now perfected. She unwittingly became his informant.

Unlike his friends, he didn't have to go through the stress of settling local communities or for security who were the better of the thieves. As the years went by, he garnered himself a platoon of enemies; hence the need to leave the country at all costs.

In the early harmattan season of 2006 Olamide arrived at the visa office an hour earlier than anticipated, and had to wait in his car for another one hour in the heat. The air condition was bad even after two repairs. He bought a newspaper just to fan himself, but it seemed to be blowing only hot, stagnant air.

He was glad Temitope was now a British citizen, and wondered why Moses, who had been there three years before his wife, didn't have one. Olamide was fortunate to have sent most of his money across the ocean before the bank officer disappeared with £27,800, the last money he had paid into his account. He had finally reached his 12 barrels benchmark, and was going to make up his losses and leave the country immediately after.

He decided to carry out a final sweep. This time, the pay was more, the risk was higher, and he could not afford to take the regular route from the port in Warri. He had to organise a crew of people who knew the terrain. As always, he organised a new team then invited his friend Osagie, a former naval officer to go with them.

Osagie was honourably discharged a few years ago, after he lost the use of his right arm. He was glad to go with his friend from high school, and to feel the absence of urban life. His gut however, kicked against the journey. His wife told him to leave his gut in Port Harcourt.

Four days later, he asked Olamide to hire a speed boat. Olamide did. Three days later, they headed for Forcados River where the exchange of crude oil was to take place.

They were twenty miles away from Aboh in Delta state when they heard the sound of several speed boats, but dismissed it as harmless because they saw mostly women and children. When they got to the boundary of Burutu, the other boats surrounded them. By this time it was too late to mount a defence.

The leader of Olamide's team whispered in harsh tones, "Close your eyes, raise your hands!"

Most of the people in his boat had already raised their hand in surrender. On one of the other boats were three women, an old man and two boys, probably in their early teens. The two pregnant women removed the mould from their belly and were rifling through it, while a woman carrying a baby, opened her napkin bag to retrieve two guns, then handed one of them to one of the boys.

"CLOSE YOUR EYES!"

The second boy alighted from his boat, onto theirs with thin muslin cloths.

They were all bound and blindfolded then jab to move forward. Osagie was counting; they travelled two hours on boat, with a few manoeuvres. After walking for thirty seven minutes, they travelled by canoe for a whole day. Each of them where then led by the hand.

Osagie smiled, it was a terrain he knew too well. He knew they were in Bayelsa state from the position of the sun, and wished he had brought a map with him. He planned their escape and wondered if the huge young man with them was much of a weightlifter or if he just looked like one. He managed to tip one side of his blindfold, and was caught.

Olamide didn't know what their kidnappers wanted, who they were, or why they were taken. Then he heard something that sounded like beating followed by a gun shot. Olamide peed in his trousers. When his blindfold was removed an hour later, he saw Osagie in front of him with his face double its size.

Olamide swallowed hard, holding his breath when he was about to choke. He slanted a look to his right and saw most of the men were fully armed. Their guns were sophisticated; the ones held by the policemen he used to come with were nothing to compare. They were all blindfolded again. There was another rap of bullets, then a tumult of whistling, following sequentially like music. He heard rapid footsteps, then everything was silent.

When he opened his eyes and saw his wife, he fainted. She poured water over him. When he woke up this time she was squatting over him.

"What are you doing here? So you are behind my kidnapping?"

"Shut up! If it was me, you'd be dead now. Wicked man, so because you wanted to marry another woman, you pushed me to go abroad, something I kicked against for years. Do I look like a trophy wife? Abi I resemble firewood?"

"I'm sorry," he replied, sounding remorseful.

She let out a long hiss, and clucked her tongue. She was too tired to fight. All she wanted was a long sleep; she had not had the time to rest since she arrived in the country four hours ago. She slumped on the ground beside him, trying to hold her head up while he helped one of the men she came with untie Osagie.

Olamide came to her side, "Are you okay?"

"Do I look okay? I followed you. Since when did you start this business? Ah!? So your plan was to make me a widow abi?"

"I'm sorry!"

She stared sternly at him.

They were about to head back after the men had given their okay, when they heard another rap of gunfire, this time in rapid succession. Olamide and Osagie remained flat on the ground, rooted to their spot. While they were trying to decipher where the sound was coming from, Temitope had started running deeper into the thicket of mangroves. Everywhere was suddenly quiet except for the sound of light footsteps. Olamide got up, tilted his head, and waited until it faded.

"Temi, I think they are gone o!" Olamide whispered. When he didn't hear her respond, he started to shiver. He spun. She was nowhere to be found. He began to panic.

Osagie saw the imprint of *Skechers* on the ground and followed it while Olamide and the others tagged along, not wanting to be left behind. Osagie was looking down and frowning, when he saw the reflection of something falling down. He turned around, and found nothing. Wondering if shock could trigger hallucination, he sighed and almost fell from shock when he saw a hand come out of the ground.

He would have ignored it or confirmed his theory if he didn't recognise his watch; Olamide won it over at their last poker game. Olamide disappeared again just as the others caught up with them. Osagie caught him by the watch, two of the men came to his side, one wrapped his hand around Osagie's waist, and the other stood beside Osagie in half-squat. Two joined the man behind Osagie with the last holding the last man, a weightlifter, held the man in front of him by the belt, and used his free hand to hold onto the mangrove stalks.

Olamide was unconscious by the time he was brought out and had to be carried on a stretcher made of their shirts and bamboo stalks.

They emptied the remaining water on his face, and threw the bottle away.

"What about recycling?" The weightlifter asked.

Everyone laughed.

Osagie frowned down at Olamide. Then he produced a mud covered compass from his pocket, shook it, and angrily tossed it. He looked at the sun, then used his hand as a sundial. He tugged Olamide's watch off, and wiped the surface, before checking the time, to determine how lost they were from the position of the sun.

Olamide seemed to be suddenly full of life and jumped, hopped, and scratched, and wriggled. Osagie instructed him on how to remove leeches, but he continued with his twisted dance steps. Everyone else shook with laughter.

Olamide attempted to walk ahead of Osagie, but was pulled back just in time to dodge another quicksand. They looked anxiously around, trying to make out where they were. Olamide wished he had paid attention to map reading in geography class.

"Where are we?" Olamide asked.

"Am I a compass? What did you get me into?"

"Don't make up excuses for being here because you got yourself into this mess."

"Hey!" Osagie said, facing his friend squarely, "Watch your mouth."

"I...I..." Olamide tripped over his tongue with embarrassment.

"I...I... what? Ol'boy no just make me vex o! No be you and Bernard dey do una deals?"

Olamide opened his mouth, then closed it, blinked and swallowed when he remembered how Osagie used to beat him back then. He lost track of how they became close friends.

Osagie suggested following the crushed leaves and disturbances in the mangrove.

They finally found Temitope. She lay sprawled in a recovery position. He and Osagie sat down beside her. Then some people came to meet her.

"How come?" Olamide asked Temitope, still scratching.

"Ah! Where is your trouser?" she asked, frowning.

"Hey!" taken aback and continued, "Where is my trouser?" then to his wife, "Who are these people?"

"They are from the village, em... it's a long name, but it's just a mile off.

"How do we get out of here?" The weightlifter asked, suddenly.

The other men stared at him then shook their heads.

"Let's check for the closest police station." The weightlifter continued.

"Eh!?" Olamide exclaimed.

Osagie nodded his approval, ignoring Olamide's attempt at getting his attention quietly.

"Don't be stupid. Don't you see the footpath leads to a village? Carry your house!" Osagie said, slapping Olamide's hand off his arm.

Olamide wrapped his arms around Temitope and she shrugged it off. "Don't you dare touch me, you useless man."

"What did I do *sef*?" he grumbled.

"You will know when we get out of here. Don't worry eh. You will know."

♥♥♥

Three weeks later, Olamide's plan to leave the country had been finalised. He had been unable to sleep properly since the incident. He didn't want to go anywhere, but Temitope's nagging gave him the courage he needed to leave the house. She suggested that he go to a therapist, and he thought she was mad to have mentioned it. His dreams were filled with quicksand; even his children were in quicksand.

One evening, as he was murmuring and hugging himself his driver came in. His driver would have ignored him, but for the fact that he had never seen his boss sit on the ground, even when he played with his daughters.

"Oga, any problem?"

"I could literally feel the sand eat me, slowly, slowly. It was like cement caking around my chest. Can you imagine that? I couldn't breathe; you know they tried to dig me out of that makeshift grave?" Olamide muttered, striking his chest.

His driver shook his head and nodded even though he didn't know what his boss was on about.

Osagie was already in Stratford, a week earlier, to see one of his cousins, Bernard, who had vowed not to come back home after he had been kidnapped twice. Bassey's wedding was taking place in less than a week and Olamide needed to be on time for the bachelor's party if he and Moses were commencing business before the end of the fiscal year.

He hadn't been able to sleep two nights before, and he drank sleeping pills which hadn't started working until now.

When he woke up it was fifteen minutes to four, he bolted up right, picked his car keys. He drove to the bank in his pyjamas – his account officer had gotten used to his many phases; so far as she was concerned he was bipolar.

Olamide was daydreaming about staying in England.

"Sir," the account officer called.

"Yes, yes," he replied quickly, blinking.

"Are you all right?"

"Yes...."

"It's just that I've been calling your attention and ..."

"I'm fine," he responded, coldly.

He found her annoying, and it infuriated him that she was the one woman that got away, with her long endless legs, curves like *Beyoncé*, and teeth that reminded him of his first crush: Amanda. Amanda, who had unknowingly caused problems in his marriage so much so that Temitope wanted to confront her, thinking her husband was sleeping with her. She finally got to Amanda, and left her crest on the poor woman: three cuts and six stitches - this, with the timely intervention of their driver, who in turn lost his job for interfering.

His account officer was honest and efficient, judging from his carelessness of late. He tried his luck at asking her out again. She flashed him a smile, and then showed off her left hand with a large ring on the ring finger. He mumbled and walked out with his money. When he got to the front desk, he grimaced and went to put some money into his account officer's personal account.

Feeling sleepy as he drove, he pushed the gear and headed home.

Olamide woke up sweating. He looked at his side, but Tcmitope wasn't there. A few minutes of hysteria reminded him of her abandoning him at home as soon as he recovered from his wounds. He climbed out of bed, took a long cold shower, and with a towel around his waist, then made a few calls but was unsuccessful: it was the weekend so none of his mistresses were available. He got up, and went to the French window. With hands resting on his waist, he wondered what UK would be like.

His towel fell off his waist. He bent down to pick it up but it wasn't on the ground. The lamp at the bedside wasn't working - he had forgotten to fix it. He grunted and stalked to the socket near the door. He turned the light on and sighed. He turned around to find Stella, his maid, sprawled on his bed with his towel on her.

Four

She didn't bother to take a test. After an ultrasound scan, she calculated backwards, deciding to abort it; there was no way it was her husband's. All she wanted was a doctor to get rid of it before her husband arrived the following week. He had left for Birmingham, and then he'd head for Southampton to see Osagie before they headed for Bassey's bachelor party. The closest appointment was in four days and that would give her two days to rest.

She woke up late on the day of the appointment feeling uneasy, but her marriage came first, and she was going to go ahead with her plan.

After achieving what she went for, she headed home relieved and light headed.

She had to think fast after she opened the door and her husband's *Cool Water* by *Davidoff* hit her; he was supposed to be back from Southampton in two days giving her time to recuperate. She started walking slowly, holding her head in her hand, with the other hand on her stomach; she stalked into the house, completing the farce with a gloomy face.

"Where have you been?" he asked. Then his anger turned to concern when she staggered and slumped. He caught her on time, carrying her to the nearest chair. There she burst into tears. Confused, he held her until she calmed down.

"I lost the baby." Temitope whispered, and burst into another bout of tears; this time it was real. The tears weren't because of the pregnancy, but because she couldn't tell her husband that she had a one night stand and the pregnancy wasn't his. She only wished she could tell him; that way she could have continued in the pregnancy. Sadly, now that she had mustered the courage, there was no pregnancy.

She cried for weeks, and Olamide's presence only worsened it. She walked like a moron around the house for days. On one occasion, she sat on the settee, her eyes focused on the coral centre piece, but her thoughts were haywire.

She wanted to keep the pregnancy; she needed to have another baby. She would have kept it if she had made up her mind on divorcing Olamide. She wondered if it was a boy. Upon hearing the doorbell chime, it occurred to her that she hadn't prepared dinner. Sighing, she reluctantly went to answer the door, wishing for once, that her daughters would use their own keys.

Ihinòsé stood at the door, smiling.

Temitope leaned on the door then grimaced, "What do you want?"

"Won't you let me in first? These shoes are tight, you know," she spat her gum out. Temitope watched as the gum landed on the petal of a red and orange false oxlip and hit the ground while Ihinòsé pushed past her.

"Mtchew." Temitope sized her friend up, and went back into the house, forgetting to close the door.

"What do you want?"

"You! Got it?" Ihinòsé laughed, removed her shoes, and massaged her toes.

Temitope hissed.

"Enough with the hissing, na wa o! What did I do this time? Abeg, if you don't want me to stay, just say so."

Temitope crossed her arms around her chest. She managed a tight lipped smile, after all Ihinòsé's company was better than none.

♥♥♥

Athena could almost feel the pores of her skin open, hungrily seeking a breath of fresh cool breeze. Unable to bear the heat any longer she walked into the kitchen in search of lemonade or anything cold. When she got to the kitchen, she forgot what she wanted the electric kettle for, and put it down. She leaned towards the door that was ajar, stumbling over some tubers of yam, but it was too late to retreat when she heard her name mentioned in the conversation. Fortunately, they were oblivious of her.

"Why did you even invite her?"

"I didn't, Ime did. Besides, the comings and goings in this house are none of your business," Joan replied.

"Who is Ime?" a woman dressed in neon coloured stirrups asked.

"She is white, you know that, abi?" spat the lady in a purple tie and dye shirt-dress.

"Are you jealous? Eh? Ihinòsé, are you?" Temitope asked, settling into one of the wicker chair, and got up almost immediately to answer another call.

Ihinòsé hissed, then started typing into her Blackberry.

"I heard they went on a cruise last year, is it true? The *ou* is handsome I hear." Serafina said, as she eked out the coleslaw unto her plate of salad.

"Yes." Temitope startled everybody with her reappearance.

"You need to stop doing that *abeg*." Tombra, a heavily pregnant woman said, rubbing her lower back at the same time.

"Ah-ah!" exclaimed Chika, another heavily pregnant woman. "My heart was already in my mouth just now."

"Heavens! Will you stop that already," Wenendah stammered.

"Who is Ime?" the woman in neon stirrups asked again not interested in Temitope's intrusion.

"My cousin. She's over there," Joan murmured pointing at a lady lounging by the pool.

"Oh! Sorry, Hi I'm Emilia." Joan's cousin waved at them and plug on an earpiece.

"Stop doing what?" Temitope asked innocently.

"Startling us, that's what! My friend, who has been distracting you?" Toyosi asked Temitope.

"Toyosi, stay out of my business," Temitope said quietly.

Toyosi! Moses has mentioned that name before. If she is here, Caroline will not be far off. Poor girls; they don't even know he has had a go with both of them and Caroline's elder sister, Emilia.

"What business? The type women do behind their husband's back?" Caroline asked.

Temitope stiffened, then turned to face her friend fuming.

Athena kept a safe distance. She was equally amused that they noticed Temitope but didn't notice her.

"Who is she talking to?" Temitope asked, pausing. "Emilia, no be you I dey talk to?"

"Shebi that is the woman you are talking about, ehen ask her nawh!" Emilia said, irritated.

""You sef!" Caroline hissed and clapped her hand in her friend's face like she was killing a bug.

"Caroline don't 'you sef' me. I find it offensive," Emilia muttered.

"Would you know 'offensive' if it stared you in the face?" Caroline asked, in a low voice before clucking her tongue.

"Una dey see as trouble dey take start o! Hmn..." Emilia mumbled something unintelligible, and bent over the table to pick up her champagne flute. She accidentally knocked Toyosi's drink over Caroline's burnt-orange dress: her apology stuck in her throat.

Caroline looked at her angrily.

Joan took the champagne bottles away from the table. Toyosi carried the remaining glasses and accidentally spilled some liquid on her tie and dye shirt-dress.

Caroline smirked the entire time: Two years ago she was in a relationship with Moses; at least that is what she thought until she saw him making out with Emilia, her sister and so called best friend, in her house. A part of her still wished she hadn't flaked out at the last minute and missed her flight. She yearned for him; who wouldn't? He came from a good background, was rich and a looker and most importantly, he knew how to take care of a woman.

Meanwhile, Athena braced herself in readiness to join the gang when she heard....

"So what does he want with a white woman that a black woman can't give him, eh?" Emilia spat.

"One thing is sure, you're not that woman." Caroline laughed gregariously, dusting her neon leggings.

"How dare you?" Emilia leans forwards banging a non-existing table with her fist.

"Oh please! Get over it, both of you!" Joan's voice rose with each word.

"Look who's talking.... you lesbian trout." Toyosi spat with contempt, still angry that Joan Imaobong ran to their neighbours after turning down her offer of intimacy. Joan, for a nanosecond, lost her balance.

"No, Joan is not a lesbian but has lesbian friends," another lady, who had been on the phone since they arrived said.

Emilia nudged the lady, "Onome.... how you take know? Because such an accusation is too much for wild imagination."

"Some people should be quiet before the cat is out of their bag." Caroline's voice was rich with satisfaction, and a mischievous smile played on her lips.

"Why do you think I'm a lesbian? And you, Onome, which of my friends are lesbians?" Joan dropped the ice bucket carclessly.

Onome shrugged, "I had to defend you."

"Look here, your clandestine activities are in my palm, here...sce...right here," Emilia said, tapping her right index finger in the middle of her left palm. "You come here with your holy holy attitude, feigning glory. Please oh!"

Caroline, Serafina and Toyosi started shifting uncomfortably.

"Are you all right?" Temitope asked Caroline. Her touch made Caroline jump, but she regained her composure immediately.

"Everybody shut up! What clandestine affair – "

"She said activities Joan. Not affairs!" Onome corrected.

"I don't see why a moth thinks it can frolic with butterflies just because it has wings." Ime said scornfully, and continued to eye Onome.

"I know you're not referring to me."

Ime pulled a towel and draped it around her waist "Who else will I be referring to, *donatus* like you."

"Oh please! Are you a lesbian or not?"

"I'm not going to justify that with an answer."

"Answer *abi*?" Caroline asked, smugly.

Temitope stood up with arms akimbo and glared at every one. "Well enough! But of you, enough! Don't you see that Joan has lost weight or even notice the wig she is wearing?"

"Temi, please don't, I beg you, don't!" Joan held her hands together like she was praying.

"Don't?"

Ime flounced over to Temitope, trying to prevent her from talking.

"Don't what?" Temitope asked, irritated. "You want me to just sit down and listen to all this rubbish? Well I'm sorry! Listen all of you, the only reason Joan visits that gay couple is because she ..." she turned to Joan, telling her to adjust her wig properly.

"I wanted to buy their wigs." Joan said, solemnly.

"So what is wrong with wearing wigs?" Onome asked, petulantly.

"The reason behind the wigs is different from what you think. I've been missing these meetings of ours because I didn't know how to face you guys," Joan said.

Temitope raised her hands in frustration, eyed Ime sternly, and stood akimbo, tapping her feet in a rhythmic fashion.

Athena understood what it was about; it was like her mother all over again. She knew that long suffering look. Joan sighed deeply, slumped into a chair and burst into tears. While the other women stared in confusion, Athena went to wrap her arms around Joan.

"What did I miss here? Wetin dey hapun?" Emilia asked as she rushed back to join the group.

"I have cancer," Joan hiccupped through her tears. "I didn't want to admit it. God knows, I still want it to be a dream."

When the woman was calm, Athena got up to leave.

Caroline twirled her champagne flute as she wondered what she would do for herself, absentmindedly. She looked around until her eyes caught something which drew her attention: Athena.

"I have to go now before I drink too much," Temitope said.

Tombra looked surprised, "Since when?"

Everyone laughed.

"Since I have to be sober to welcome my kids." Temitope started to laugh loudly. Ime shook her head then after collecting Temitope's car keys, decided to give her a lift.

"I'm sorry. I only wanted you to have fun while Moses was away," Ime said.

"I know. Why didn't you tell me?"

Ime shrugged.

Temitope brushed past them. Joan caught her arm on time before she went crashing into the chairs in the opposite direction. *See, someone that would have been taking care of me after chemo.* "Temitope, this is Athena, Moses' wife, and this is Olamide's wife."

"Oh hi!"

"Hi!" Temitope said, smiling sweetly and giggling. "I've been meaning to meet you."

"Me too, but I've got to go."

"Me too, my kids you know."

"How many?"

"Two little girls. Well... they aren't so little anymore."

Joan bundled Temitope into the back seat of the Toyota Camry in case she puked and handed the keys to Ime.

"Not a good day, yeah?" Temitope asked, as soon as Athena fasten her seatbelt.

Athena shrugged, "I can't say for sure."

"Why don't you come to mine for dinner?" Temitope dug her hand into her bag to search for her keys but her hand-eye coordination was at its least.

"Oh no, I don't want to be a bother."

"Oh, don't be silly."

"Okay, but don't say I didn't warn you 'cause I may not be a good enough company."

"Don't worry I'll take you out of your blues."

♥♥♥

The door slammed shut. School bags tumbled to the ground in heavy thuds, and the creaking of the floor board announced the return of her daughters. Her shoulders sagged as the thought of the baby crossed her mind.

The 'how was school?' was followed by shrugs then 'won't you give your mum a hug?' followed by a perfunctory hug. She sighed, then murmured, "It's better than nothing." Taiwo produced the two litre jug of orange juice from the apple green American fridge while Kehinde brought out the cake their mother had baked early in the morning.

She watched them from the sitting room, smiling proudly, before turning her attention back to Athena.

"I'm glad they are eating."

"Hmn?!"

"You see, they were really distracted for weeks until two days ago. I think it may have been a crush or something like that."

Athena stared at Kehinde's plate, bewildered. "Don't you think that is too much food for one meal?"

Temitope looked at Athena intently and muttered, "You're a beautiful woman. No wonder he married you."

Athena blushed.

Five

When they got to the till, Moses went back into the store to get more drinks in preparation for the event they were hosting the following day. Athena's phone rang. Frowning, she pressed the green button. "Hello!" She spoke into the receiver, balancing the phone between her shoulder and her left cheek while she put their supplies in the bag.

"Who is this?" a female voice asked, in an unpleasant tone.

"I beg your pardon?" Her voice was slightly raised with irritation.

"Can you please give the phone to Moses?" the voice from the other end said with contempt.

"I'm sorry you are mistaken, this is my phone."

"Give the phone to its owner, will you?" The other person raised her voice.

She stopped packing groceries into the bag, held the phone away, and stared at it in dismay. She could still hear the voice on the other end when she pressed the red button. She shoved it back into her jeans then. She resumed what she was doing, ignoring the phone as it rang. She shrugged off the curious stare of the other customers that lined up behind her.

"Are we set?" Moses asked, rubbing his forehead with the back of his thumb.

"I guess we are!" Athena replied with an upturned smile. He didn't like her tone, but wasn't in the mood for a conversation. He pushed the trolley through the park to their *Mercedes Benz Avant-garde coupe CLK 500* – a wedding gift - and insisted that she stayed in the car while he put their shopping in the booth. As she opened the door to enter the car, his phone rang. Curiously, she left the door slightly open. He looked to her direction when it rang the second time.

"Hello!" Moses said into the phone as he tried to see what his wife was doing.

"Hi!"

"Sorry, who is this?" Moses asked, tilting his heard slightly to check on his wife. Then he backed away from the car.

Athena looked at him from the rear view window.

"Hi! It's me Megan, are you all right?"

"Yes. Why?" he said, while toying with the leaves from the shrub beside him.

"I need to speak with you! It's important."

"I'll tell you where to meet."

"I miss you!"

"I miss you too!" he said, lowering his voice.

"Will you call me later?"

"I'll try."

"I love you!"

"I love you too." Moses turned around. He froze and simultaneously dropped his phone.

Athena sized her husband up, poised her lips, and picked up the phone, scrutinizing it. She shook her head when she found just a little scratch on it. After wiping it off, she handed it out to him smiling, but he seemed suddenly reluctant to collect it from her.

"I seem to be startling you a lot these days. I'm sorry love but it's fun to see you can be squeamish," she said.

"Oh yeah?" he laughed nervously. He was actually a little relieved that she didn't hear his conversation from her reaction.

"Uh-huh!" Athena tried to shrug off his discomfort with a laugh.

"Come here!" He pulled her so hard she hit him squarely, and he staggered. He lifted her face up with his hands touching her lips lightly with his thumb. She shivered slightly as she sniffed in the calm spring breeze.

"Let me take you home."

After they had stacked the groceries in the various cabinets, she ordered pizza, but she couldn't stand the smell of the pizza. Deciding that it was something in that particular pizza, she settled for the garlic bread. There was no space in the fridge to store the remaining pizza; Moses turned it into the bin while she took the cookery to the sink. She could feel his eyes on her.

"Hon..., are you okay?" He turned to his left to see her.

"Yeah!" Her back was still turned to him.

"It's just that you didn't eat your pizza and that's not like you. Is what the Doctor said bothering you?" he leaned on her, wrapping his arms around her.

She held his arms in place for a while. He released her abruptly when she leaned into him so that he could go to the fridge. There he lingered for a few seconds. Then he came back, and pulled her into his arms. She sighed; *I miss this!* They both danced to a song that only he could hear because their steps were not aligned as he kept stepping on her: these were steps he knew even in his sleep. He stiffened for a nanosecond and was no longer dancing when his second phone rang. She looked at the clock behind him; it was eleven fifteen. *Who can it be?*

He picked it up, and gave her a slanted look.

She pretended not to notice.

"Hello? hold on..."

She opened her mouth to say something, but changed her mind. After stalling for a few minutes, he stalked out of the kitchen. She watched him leave. For the past two months, all she could do to his change in attitude was sigh deeply. He was out more often now, not that it was a problem, except that they no longer went out together; even though she never liked those monotonous socialite events that ended up dismissing her positive vibe.

He missed every appointment they had with the doctors. As if that wasn't enough, they argued incessantly about the littlest things, from the calls that he received late in the night, or the work he brought back home, to the position of the toothpaste because she squeezed from the middle. He had been spoiling for a fight of late, and it was no use discussing anything with him. This call she could bet was from the same woman that called her over two hours ago.

She sighed heavily, wiped her hand on the tea towel, and placed everything she had washed on the drain. Taking one last look at everything, she went to bed.

She tossed and turned for hours, and when he finally came in to lie beside her, she pretended to be asleep. She was silently crying; feeling worse than she did when she was single and trying to get her mother off her back. This time the weight did overwhelm her, and worse, there was no one to unburden on or with.

She thought of going on a vacation, but chances were that he would bring that girl into their home – something she discovered a lot of African men did. The annoying part in any decision she wanted to make were the words of Nadine's mother bugging her every now and then. 'A woman with no husband is no woman at all!' her best friend Nadine's mum used to say before she died.

Nadine was the most annoying, frustrating, and most obnoxious girl she had ever met. Initially, she tolerated her because she was lonely, and needed someone to talk to. She was not allowed any friends back then; the first time she brought a classmate home, her mother made her study at home for two whole years.

Nadine was the housekeeper's daughter, and her mother was the only housekeeper who stayed on longer than six months. Athena didn't understand why they remained best friends to date; they had different tastes in everything. She was grateful all the same because, without her friend she would never have known what love felt like. Even though their marriage had reached a trying tide, she wouldn't have wanted anything more.

♥♥♥

"I'm sorry, but you lost the pregnancy." The doctor's words still echoed in Temitope's head. *How could I be pregnant, and not even know it?* She picked up her diary and daily planner and began to calculate. She was satisfied at the third run-through that she had seen her period, but she didn't feel confident. They'd been trying to get pregnant for a long time. She had almost given up, but Olamide was hopeful.

She wasn't in the mood to be dour so she played some light music while she watched a movie. Then ordered pizza, which arrived forty minutes later, giving her enough time to take her prescription and stack up her activities for the following day. Remembering how she fainted the last time she decided to toast a slice of bread while she waited. Feeling a little disturbed, she opted to calling her husband to tell him what happened.

"Hello!" a female voice drawled from the other end.

She frowned, ended the call, and redialled the number.

"Hello!" It was the same voice, but purring this time.

"Hi! Can I speak to Olamide?"

"At this hour? He isn't here at the moment. Who's calling?" the voice went from high pitch to drawl.

"His wife." Temitope snarled.

"Sorry?"

"Who are you and what are you doing with my husband's phone?"

"I'm Crystal Jonas, his wife."

"His what?" Temitope screeched, standing up. She was furious. She sat down, and shook her legs vigorously. Cracking her fingers at the same time and ignoring the doorbell. Tired of hearing the chiming of the doorbell, she went to answer it. She told the pizza delivery boy to wait while she went to fetch her purse. Not watching where she was going, she accidentally knocked down the flower vase on the sideboard, but caught it in time. A thumbs-up shaped post-it fell as she replaced the vase. When she bent down to pick up the post-it, an idea occurred to her. She rummaged for a pen in one of the drawers in the sideboard.

Soon after the delivery boy left, she plastered the post it on the door which read:

Go back to Crystal Jonas, your new wife.

She locked the door, climbed upstairs, and fell into a fitful sleep.

A few hours later, the pain in her lower abdomen increased waking her up. She winced as she got up to take some pills. Not bothering to turn on the light, she went to the toilet with her bag of dispensary. She took her pills. Leaning on the wall, with one hand resting on the sink, she took a deep breath.

When she turned on the light to their bedroom, she found her husband in bed. She almost kicked herself: she had forgotten about his set of keys. She went into their en suite briskly, came back and doused him with water. He jumped, tangled his feet in the sheet, and in struggling to get out of it, he hit his elbow on the side of the bed. He ended up on the ground like a live fish flapping on a hot sandy shore.

"What is it nawh?" he asked, morosely, nursing his elbow. His time in boarding school flashed through his mind.

"How did you get in here?"

"With my keys." He sulked.

"At what time?"

"Don't know, after work?"

"After work eh?"

"I work."

"Yes oh! I know! On top of women!"

"Woman, not this again!"

"I'm now 'woman' *abi*?" Woman oh! Temitope Eniola Ademinokan is now woman o!"

"For goodness sake – "

"For goodness sake *kó*, for goodness sake *ni*. Why didn't you go back to your new wife? Eh?"

"New wife?" he asked, hysterically.

"Crystal Jonas."

"What? Who the hell is that?" He frowned, giving her a slanted look.

"Think! Think hard. What line will you give me this time, Mr. Man. Think oh! Think very well!" she hissed, still clapping her hands.

"Do you know what the time is?"

"Yes oh! I haven't even started with you *sef*."

He got up, taking a dry pillow with him and headed towards the door. She got there first, and leaned in like she was posing on it.

"Get out of my way, woman!"

"Or what? Man, or what?"

"Why can't you let me be, eh?"

Temitope hissed.

Olamide went back to his side of the bed, and lay on the ground.

"Taah! You want to sleep? So you wanted to see if I'd die so that you could bring one of your *ashewo* to my house *abi*?"

"My house."

"My house. I bought it!" Temitope stood akimbo, leaning on the door.

"It's my house because I paid for it."

"I'm your wife so it's our house."

"Thank God for that." He sniggered.

"What do you mean by that? I –"

He covered her mouth with his. She fought him off until she couldn't resist him anymore, then he let her go.

"Don't touch me again," she said, slowly trying to compose herself.

"I'm sorry!" His hand brushed her cheek and each time she brushed it away.

"I'm sorry!" he repeated.

"You're not sorry. Why didn't you answer my call?"

"Temi, the battery was out, and I thought we were over this already?"

"Over, over? so... why was it ringing?"

"You know it will ring anyhow."

"That is all you have to say abi? Tomorrow somebody will say how I keep looking for his trouble, yet you look for my trouble every day. I will start to play my own too. No worry, shebi you think say na only you get prick?"

"Jesus Christ!"

"Jesus has got nothing to do with your sleeping around, so call that name with respect."

"I'm not sleeping around."

"Why didn't you pick up my call?"

"I didn't see it."

"I thought you said the phone was dead."

"That is why I didn't see it nawh! Na wa oh!" He sat at the edge of the bed.

"Why did a girl pick up your call?" She took off her dressing gown.

"My assistant is a girl isn't she?" He looked up to see her reaction.

"Yes, and I know her voice. Who is the girl o?"

"Who is the girl o?" he mimicked, trying not to stammer.

"Stop repeating what I say oh! Why did a girl pick your calls?"

"There is no way a girl could have picked... The battery was dead for goodness sake. "

"Oh! Okay oh!" She sashayed to the dressing table, then turned around with her hands tucked behind her. Unknown to him, she was dialling his number. When it started to ring, she added, "Well, there is a snag to that story then!" then she looked at him expectantly.

"My PA may have charged it for me. I honestly didn't know."

"At 1am abi?" she asked, laughing.

"Honey..." He walked towards her.

"It's no longer, 'woman'."

"Honey, see eh – "

"If you come near me eh!"

"Come on nawh!" he eyed her voluptuous chest in the see-through turquoise baby-doll lingerie she wore.

"Oya, quickly, out of this room. I want to sleep."

"Temi!" he rumbled.

"I said, get out!"

"Temi my love, you know you are my one and only oh!"

"Shebi I just told you to leave. Let nobody hear my voice this night oh! Just go!

Olamide walked towards the door and opened it, but when he saw her back was turned to him, he shut it. He went swiftly to her, spun her around, and plastered her with kisses while tugging at the strap of her lingerie.

Six

The birds were tweeting when Temitope opened her eyes. She curled her legs up when she felt a faint gust of wind touch her feet. Then she smiled to herself when last night's event flooded her thoughts. She looked at the time and decided to make breakfast for her husband before he left for squash.

She was tempted to follow him to find out what they were really 'squashing' during squash, but since she had never bothered to go she felt it unnecessarily to make an effort now. Sighing, she pulled out a pair of socks and put them on. She removed the pins that were holding her hair and let it tumble down her back. *This is for you!* She didn't like letting her hair down unless it was too short to curl up.

She hummed all the way to the kitchen. As she was arranging the table to place a breakfast of potato hash, scrambled eggs, toasted mushroom, potato hash, and fried buttered bread, the doorbell rang. Glad she didn't have to answer the door because Olamide was in the sitting room, she proceeded to what she was doing. She brought the water in a filter jug, and turned on the portable radio then padded to the sitting room to call him when she heard her husband say in a loud whisper.

"How did you know my house?"

"I..." the lady leaned in, and said "Hi!" waving at Temitope, who just stood behind her husband with arms akimbo, tapping her feet at the same time. "You his mum?" the lady in question asked curiously. Temitope gritted as she sized the girl up and stared daggers at her husband. She was about to scurry away to empty the food she had dished for him, and lock the kitchen when the girl said, "Not a very nice woman is she?"

Temitope's anger was now sizzling hot, "I'll show you 'not nice'". She shoved her husband, and pushed the door open at the same time. The girl backed away as Temitope approached her. Olamide intercepted his wife before she could get to the girl's dress which was less than an inch out of her reach. She stomped her heels on her husband's foot. He groaned in pain, but refused to let her go.

"Look at this chicken o! Do I look like your mother?"

"If you're indeed his sister, you should be shipped to a sanatorium."

"What? Olamide o, this witch just called me a mad woman, and you're still holding me abi?"

"Ola-a why don't you do something to muffle this nuisance 'cause I need to come in." the lady said, gesturing at Temitope.

"In where? My house? I don suffer. OLAMIDE!" she shouted biting her index finger. "So this is Crystal Jonas eh?"

"Sorry, it's Katherine Ferdinand." The girl said, wearing a smug look.

"Oh you're number two. Ah! You came to be buried. I say, you came to be buried." She lunged at the lady, but her husband tilted her so that his back was turned to the girl. "Mr. Man if you don't leave me now you'll be the one that will be buried, I promise you!" Temitope hissed.

The girl let out a throaty laugh.

"See, this one wen oyibo don reject," Temitope said, scratching her head. She jumped and clawed at Olamide. "Olamide, I swear if you don't let me go, you'll be the one that will be buried oh!"

When he didn't answer, she scratched him with her newly manicured French tips. He didn't let her go, so she dug her nails in his hand and kicked him in his crotch. He let her go and they fell. By the time she had regained her balance, the girl had disappeared. She locked the gate, and stalked back into the house.

"Ah Olamide, you've finished me. Eh? Other people's dustbin you'll go and visit. I swear to God, if you give me a disease you will wish you were dead oh!" Olamide wasn't listening; he was gulping down the food hurriedly. "Why are you eating my food? Go, let one of your whores cook for you jó!"

He held onto the plate; while she tugged at it, he ate from it. Unable to take the plate from him, she resorted to pouring water into it then raced upstairs, and locked the bedroom door.

A few minutes later, he was banging at the door asking her for his keys – she had locked the door with his key which was already in the keyhole.

He knew she hated the shrilling sound of the smoke alarm, so he went in search of match stick, and spotted a match box in the centre piece. He wondered why she kept it there, and set off to the kitchen. He climbed onto the stool and then came back down to get paper.

He lit the paper before climbing onto the stool a second time. He blew out the fire, then waved it at the smoke alarm. He fell as the alarm's shrill sound came through. Rubbing his ear, he ran to the one in the dining room – their room was right above it- and triggered another one. Unfortunately, she had bought earplugs the day before, when she went to get her prescriptions from *Boots* because one of their neighbours was renovating their house.

Olamide's stomach growled, but the kitchen door was still locked. He was baffled at the fact that he didn't notice her go towards the kitchen. He wanted to break down the door, but he didn't want to aggravate her any further, or be doused this time with hot water. When his stomach groaned again, he went to her secret stash of chocolates.

Temitope's legs buckled underneath her. *What do I do with this man? I know one thing for sure; he will not kill me before my time.* She wanted to put a stop to it; the girls were growing more and more upfront, and she needed to nip it at the bud. She didn't want more girls to appear from nowhere to give her headaches. She smiled to herself as she remembered Ihinòsé who had been married five times in the last six years. She divorced whenever she felt their activities were too repetitive.

Temitope ransacked the whole room for about two hours before she found the lady's card. *He thinks because I allowed him to touch me that I won't deal with them? Not me nawh haha! It can't happen, not again. Two can play this game. It's time I fight. Besides I have time on my side. Phew! What to do? What to do? What to do?*

Sighing, she dialled Ihinòsé's phone number. Glad that her friend hadn't picked the call as she no longer felt like it, at that moment her phone rang. She quickly walked into the bathroom, and shut the door in case her husband was close to their bedroom.

"If it's not my feisty fr'enemy." Ihinòsé cooed from the other end.

"That is good morning abi?"

"Actually it's afternoon. Sorry dear. What's up? Is it urgent?"

"Sort of."

"Name it."

"I want to investigate someone." Temitope said, hesitantly.

"Your husband." Ihinòsé said matter-of-factly.

"Yes, my husband."

"Isn't it too late for that?"

"Can we please skip this chit chat?"

"Sure thing. When do we meet? Not today though, I'm busy."

"Busy doing what? If I may ask."

"You may not but if you must know, moonlighting. I just got another divorce."

"Well good for you." Temitope was taken aback. She was unsure of giving Ihinòsé a compliment – she didn't know her friend had remarried.

"You should try some, it's relaxing."

"Thanks, but no thanks!"

"I'll call you tomorrow. Hhm... say ten o'clock, okay?"

"In the morning, you mean?"

"Afraid?"

"No, but I wouldn't want to keep you from moonlighting," *Whatever that is!*

"With all pleasure, ciao." Ihinòsé purred.

♥♥♥

Cindy looked around Moses' office; it was filled with square mannish wooden furniture unlike Olamide's office, which was plush, soft and colourful. She could feel each hair follicle on her skin stand. She was in the office of a man she had been infatuated with since she started working in the company.

She saw it as message from God that he asked her to come to his office. While she was waiting her turn to see him, she heard his voice; it was deep, though not as deep as Barry White's, but certainly deeper than Olamide's. *Has Olamide told him of our arrangement?* He had such a command that she wondered if she should simply wait till he asked her to sit. She stood with arms clasped behind her and praying that her legs would carry her until the meeting was over.

Moses perused her like he did with sensitive or financial documents. What she lacked in cleavage, she made up for in curves. She looked ordinary, but wasn't boring. He hoped she was as gullible as she looked.

"Good morning, sir." She curtsied.

"Good morning. Please don't do that again." He frowned.

"Don't do what, sir?"

"That thing... kneeling down, it's not acceptable in an office environment."

"Yes sir, it won't happen again."

"Sit."

"Sorry?"

"Sit down."

She sat down.

"I learned that you started working for us two months ago. Cindy ..."

"Cindy Badmus, sir."

"Cindy Badmus," he said, nodding like he was counting each letter in her name. "I don't make it a point of duty to get acquainted with the staff of this company so I'll cut to the chase. Excuse me!" he paused. "Are you nervous?"

"No, Sir!" she said in a faint voice.

"Good. I know you are Mr. Ademinokan's Personal Assistant. I'll be expecting your discretion in this matter."

"Okay, sir."

"Why don't you sit down?" he gestured to the sofa at one end of the room, then sat opposite her.

Cindy found it hard to sit comfortably and sat at the edge of the chair.

"Would you like something to drink, Coffee, tea?"

"I'm fine. Thank you sir!" she could hear a dull sound in her chest.

"Well Cindy, is it okay... is it okay if I call you by your first name."

"Yes sir," she whispered, then repeated it a little too loud.

"Are you all right?"

She nodded. "Yes sir!"

"As you may well know, I have no children of my own." He paused.

"God's time is the best, sir."

"Yes, absolutely. But remember, heaven does help those who help themselves."

"I don't understand, sir!" She stuttered anxiously.

"Why don't you call me Moses for now, hmn?"

"Okay sir," lowering her voice she added, "Moses."

"That's better. I have a proposition for you!"

She nodded.

I will pay you a hundred thousand pounds before and after our transaction. Your discretion is required. Whether you accept what I'm requesting of you... it must not leave the room."

She nodded.

He pretended not to notice. "Are we in agreement?"

She looked up, "Yes sir."

"I want a girl who will be something like a surrogate, if you get my meaning."

"No, I don't sir." She tucked her palms underneath her thighs as they were now shaking.

"Yes, you do. If you were to get pregnant..."

"Sir!" Cindy exclaimed, getting up. Then she sat back down slowly. *Insemination, I heard it's a painful process. I need this money o! What have I got to lose anyway? What about Ty? But, we need the rent like yesterday!*

"I will pay you the second half as soon as the baby is in my care. I'm an old fashioned man..." he said, cutting through her thought. "I believe in doing the services, you catch my drift, yes?"

She cleared her throat, "Can I ease myself sir?"

The phone buzzed; he picked it up, nodded at Cindy and pointed at the lavatory. Irritated, he spoke into the phone. "Yes Andrew, what can't wait?"

"Mr. Ademinokan is here to see you."

Before he could ask to be excused, Cindy ran into the toilet. He thought it was because of what he told her.

"Olamide, what's up? Came to look for your PA?"

"No. She called in sick, Why?"

"I wanted to speak to her."

"Why?" Olamide asked nervously.

"Nothing serious. Her name sounded familiar."

"Oh! Why not ask Andrew to find out for you?"

"I think I'll do just that. Sit down."

"Sort of in a hurry, I stopped by because Temitope insisted you and your missus come over for dinner. Need to discuss something with you, but I have to get to the bank first."

"Bank?"

"Something's wrong with my account or my card, need to check it out."

"When is dinner this time?" Moses laughed.

"On time. Stupid man!" he chuckled before exiting.

Soon after he left, Cindy came out. She pulled out a pen from its holder, scribbled on his notepad, and left.

Amused, Moses picked it up, she had written her address.

♥♥♥

As Athena's car swooped past the uncongested road, she didn't have time to gulp in the serene beauty of a place that looked like something out of a painting; the cascading hills, tall brown trees which flanked both sides of the road with their first bloom of floret, a declaration of spring's approach. Most of them had shrubs lining it. She nearly swerved off the road when she saw a large patch of yellow field, and wondered what it was. Fortunately, the foul smell of cow dung brought her mind back to the road.

The road was narrow, and looked like a one-way route. She hadn't seen any car for the past two hours except for the red Pinto which was hiccupping down the road, and the pink and white small pickup van. The last street sign she saw was thirty minutes ago. The sat-nav didn't seem to recognize where she was, and she couldn't afford to admit that she was lost.

She hit the sat-nav; she didn't feel like talking to anyone, especially not today, but if she was actually lost she would have to.

"Oh no!"

The car started making a sound like a train coming to a stop, and came to a halt. She turned the key, but the car refused to start. She got out of the car, and raising the bonnet like someone who knew what to do. She stared at it, irritated that she knew nothing about cars. She banged it shut and looked around. She kept a hand over her eyes to shield them from the blazing sun, which did nothing to dissipate the chill in the wind.

If only there was a filling station nearby! Why didn't I just ask for directions earlier? Now I'm in the middle of nowhere with a hopeless car. She went back to staring at the car like a bully spoiling for a fight with a child who didn't scare easily.

It didn't look like people lived anywhere around there. She went back to the car, bending over the driver's seat to retrieve her phone from her brown and black *Jimmy Choo* tote on the passenger side of the car. *What is that number that is always in your face on TV?* She couldn't think of a number to call in this kind of situation and, to worsen it, the service bar was down to one. Leaning on the car, she tapped her phone on her chin.

From a distance, a woman pulling her shopping trolley came towards her. The woman was thin and looked frail; her dark blue winter jacket looked like it had seen better days, but her chocolate brown boots looked fairly new, with her hair in a tight chignon, she walked tall. Since Athena had met many ebony women who were loud, sneaky, and sometimes shifty, she was sceptical to ask her for directions, although this one was an old woman. *She seems simple enough.*

"Hi! Hello!" Athena shouted, waving her hand at the woman who was now on the opposite side of the road.

The woman looked at her, frowned, and continued her journey for a few seconds; finally stopping, turned to face Athena. Athena crossed the road to meet the woman, who looked hesitant. *She's probably unwilling to help me, I don't blame her.*

"Hi!" Athena smiled, nervously.

"Are you all right?" the woman asked, sounding concerned.

"Yes...I'm...I don't know where I am..." Athena suddenly felt embarrassed, "...and my car has broken down."

"What a pity! Well I can't help you there." The woman said, firmly.

"Where is this?" Athena asked.

The woman frowned, then raised her brow when she understood what she meant.

"I don't know my dear, I just pass through. But you are within Brackley. The next bus stop is roughly thirty minutes from here..." she said, pointing to her left. She waved her hand over her face. "...and the other is through that path behind your car about five minutes' walk."

"Where do they lead?" Athena looked behind her.

The woman shook her head and sighed, "Why don't you join me to my house, and you can call the mechanic from there."

"Hhm...." Athena shrugged, "Thank you!"

"I know these places because I usually go for a walk with my son. He loves long walks." She took a long look at Athena, "Take off your jewelleries and that bag. Put them in here." The woman gave her a wrinkled white cellophane bag with the British Heart Foundation logo on one side.

"Thank you!"

"You're a polite one, aren't you?" *Hard to find these days!*

Athena nodded her thanks, and followed the woman.

The woman's house looked dilapidated. A pile of red bricks was used to make up for the missing steps, which had rotted away. The smell that hit Athena almost knocked her out when the woman opened the door. There was someone on the large sofa, but she couldn't make out the figure. It was all covered with a large faded blue and green cloth. The woman peeled it off of the person. He mumbled, grimaced, then got up in agony and went through a door next to the open-plan kitchen.

Athena gasped as she caught sight of the exquisite details of the house; the arch was sculptured like the architectures she saw when she visited Prague. She found that the smell of burning wood was soothing, and was enthralled by the fireplace. As she watched the wood crackle in the fire, the rare sight of real, yellow, little waves of flame reminded her of the first and only campfire she had - when her father was still alive. Above the fire place was a large mirror with a frame that looked like something from the *Shire*. *This house must have been beautiful once!*

"I'm sorry about my son...." The woman looked in the direction the boy had gone. She held the blanket to her chest, sighing as she folded it with pain in her eyes. "....the phone is there." The woman turned away from Athena, pointing at the wall in the kitchen at the same time.

Athena tried to be polite. She didn't want to show her distaste for the dirtiness of the house, so she turned slightly to check on the woman. Noticing that the woman wasn't looking, she pulled out a Kleenex tissue from her pocket, and quickly wiped the phone before using it.

"Thank you!" she said after making the call.

The woman gestured.

Athena closed her eyes, and took a deep breath before she sat down. The woman noticed this and smiled. "Probably never met a poor and untidy person before...."

Athena turned red with embarrassment, but liked the fact that the woman said it kindly.

"I can't clean the house with a sick son." The woman picked up some dust covered books, sneezing.

"Where did you get these? They are lovely." Athena surprised, smoothing down the cushion.

"I made them, and thanks for the compliment." The woman replied, amused at the change in Athena's voice.

"Will you teach me? Please!"

"Okay!" *I could use the money!*

They talked for about an hour before a knock on the door reminded them of the time. The woman went to answer it, then called her. They went with the mechanic to her car. It was five-thirty by the time the mechanic finished. The traffic hold-up was so bad that she did an hour's journey in four and half hours. Moses was already at home, sprawled on a sofa, twirling a glass of gin.

Seven

"Hi Hon."

"Where are you coming from?" Moses slanted a look at her.

Athena took off her shoes. "Where do I start from?" Athena laughed, walking towards him with open arms.

"You now answer my question with another question?" he asked in a harsh tone, pushing her away from him.

She plopped down on the chair, taken aback "What do you want me to say?"

"You're doing it again." Moses raised his voice.

Doing what again? "I'm sorry!" She rubbed her aching feet. He had been on the verge for the past two weeks. She wondered if it had to do with the woman that had been calling him lately.

"Sorry? Is that all you have to say?"

Athena opened her mouth to say something, but shut it back. She held her breath to control her pacing heartbeat. At the same time she determined what to say that wouldn't further incite an argument. Athena already at her wits end asked. "Can I prepare you something to eat?"

"At this time?" Pointing at the Rolex she gave as a wedding gift.

Athena bit her lips to fight back tears and asked quietly, "What do you want me to do?"

"Why are you suddenly keen on what I want? Have you done something I need to know about?" Moses dropped the bottle of rum hard on the coffee table. He tried to steady himself as he got up.

"What do you want from me?" She asked, trying to control herself.

"Go on. Try to cover your steps." He got up quickly, spilling his drink on the white rug, which she had spent the early hours of the day cleaning.

"Are you fucking kidding me? Seriously? How about you tell me what you've been up to?" She leaned towards him, breathing heavily.

"Hey! You're the one who has been out for hours now." Moses moved his hands like someone making a presentation, still trying to keep his feet on the ground.

"You're all right, huh? Trying to play one of your flimsy schemes on me..." She sniggered. "How about you let me in on your tricks, because I'm *so* stupid, ey? So far you've not been off your game..." she said, fuming.

"You don't get to talk to me like that." He covered the space between them in a matter of seconds, and grabbed her, pulling her to him. She tried, in vain, to tear herself away from his grip.

"Take your fucking hands off me! What the hell?" she shouted.

He tightened his grip, "You don't get to tell me what to do either. I'm the man of the house."

"You are hurting me! What's come over you?" She asked as she tried to free herself from his grip.

Ignoring her attempts to shove him off, he kissed her roughly; then pushed her back into the chair, tearing her shirt. She fought with him as he tried to pull off her trousers. She shrieked in pain when her skin got stuck in the zipper. She was too stunned to scream, and in a matter of seconds he was out of his clothes; he used his knees to pin down her thighs. He yanked her trousers with so much force that they fell down from the sofa.

She stiffened when she realised he was already inside her. It wasn't until she heard his footsteps on the creaky floorboard on the steps that she realised he had come off her; she remained motionless throughout.

She blinked several times. Everything suddenly seemed too loud; the ticking of the clock clanked steadily, the groaning of the pipe sounded like a roaring lion. She shivered, shrugged, but it still felt the same. She covered her eyes, and plugged her ears with her fingers, but there was no difference. Her heart raced rapidly, and her breath arduous.

She heard something, afraid that he was coming back; she curled up into a foetal position, shaking. A few minutes later, she sat up slowly, and began to laugh hysterically. Then she fell silent for a while, rocking herself. *It can't be? No, it can't be!* Still dazed, willing it to have been a dream, she tried to get up, but doubled over in pain. After a few deep breaths, she tried to stand, but was still shaking so much. She felt light-headed and dizzy.

Exhausted with trying, she stretched out an unsteady hand, tugged the throw she had just bought then threw it over her body. Desperate to breath, she raised her aching body, clutching at the sofa for support. She removed her hand from the settee almost immediately as if something had stung her.

She pinched herself several times to wake up.

She rubbed the tears from her face, got up, and walked slowly into the guest room. *What did I do wrong? I have never been obstinate towards him. When was the last time he tried to satisfy me? But I have never refused him because of that, or have I? Not that I remember. Is it because I told him that he hadn't touched me in weeks? I should have kept my mouth shut. No matter what I did, we could have talked it over. After all, he is my husband. What has come over him? O God, I've certainly done something wrong!*

She had only the throw, but was afraid of wearing the clothes she had on. She wondered if it was karma dealing with her. Now, she didn't know what to think. In fact, she was afraid to. Her fingers and toes were numb even after she massaged them.

The heating in the room wasn't working, and they'd been meaning to fix it for the past six months now. She thought that she could remain there, dying of cold but she refused to give Moses the satisfaction. Besides, it would be a long and painful way to die for sure. Her ears were now numb, and her head was splitting. She praised the people that lived on the street. She had heard, read, and partially seen terrible things men did to women, but this one crowned it all. She braced herself to go get her things. She tried to avoid the creaking steps and felt like a thief.

When she got to the room, it was like she was locked up in zoo with a hungry gray-wolf; the room that once felt like a honeymoon suite at *Sandals* now felt like a lion's den. With each step she took, she thought her heart couldn't beat any faster.

Thank God he is already asleep! As if she thought too soon, he stirred turning towards her. She held her breath, her pounding heart deafening her ears. *I'm too young for a heart attack! Please God! Please God! Please God! Don't let him wake up! Please! Please! Please!* Those twenty seconds felt like two hours.

She gathered anything she could get her hands on, and turned around to leave. Then she remembered her phone, if it wasn't for the fact that Nadine would call her in a few hours, she would have totally abandoned it. It was on top of the chest of drawers on the other side of the bed. She tiptoed towards the bed with her heart in her mouth. She picked it up, carefully.

She felt like she had died and gone to hell when his hand fell on hers. She held her breath again. She counted to fifty to steady her heartbeat, which was already on overdrive. Gently, she slid her hand out of his, then went flat on the ground, before crawling to the door. It was only after she had reached the guest room, and locked herself inside that she realized she'd been crying.

She wiped her face, cracked her knuckles - a habit she had absorbed from Moses - and shuddered. She played with her fingers, unable to think or remember; her mind was blank and her body numb. She leaned back on the bed, staring at the ceiling.

She shut her eyes to stop the tears from coming back, rocking herself simultaneously. She stretched her hands out. The light from the street lamp caressed the diamond in her ring, and caused it to glisten. She turned her hand out, and glared at it. *For better or for worse; 'Til death do us apart,* she scoffed. She remembered how they met like it was yesterday: where she went to work as Nadine's substitute.

For the first time in her life, she had to take a menial job.That was six years ago. She needed to do it for her best friend, Nadine. It was a very cold winter morning. Nadine got the flu. Their rent was almost due but she didn't have any more money because she had given it all to Nadine to use as living costs for her Visa application so she had to leave the house at six-thirty that Saturday because she couldn't afford a taxi.

She was already tired after working for only thirty minutes, but then she thought about Nadine, and continued working. Since, chances were that they would both lose their house, the last thing she needed was to meet her mother, no matter what happened.

She was mopping the laminated floor and walking backwards towards the exit door when someone coming towards her from behind stuck his feet in the mop. In trying to pry his leg out of the mop, he went down, taking part of the shelf with him. She had never been so embarrassed in her life – at that time of the day, there was an influx of early morning workers - she went pink; then red, then purple in less than a second; and the man that fell, found it funny.

She declined his offer of a date but Nadine's boss said it was her fault, insisting that it was good PR. She, on the other hand, agreed because she wanted to see him again.

He was no shorter than five feet eight, but he stood tall in her eyes. He had brown eyes. He didn't have a pointed nose like her ex-boyfriend did but he had dimples when he smiled. He had a brilliant smile, even though she always found his teeth amusing; it was small and childlike. He had well-toned arms and abs; she could tell from the moment she checked him out after he tripped.

He scored a ten out of ten for the ability to make her laugh, even though the jokes were obviously Kevin Hart's. He turned out to be a shoulder for her to lean on, especially with her mother's third divorce wrapped around her. He got a bonus overload on her good books for being the only man who could defy her mother Cora's audacity.

At work's end, she came out of the shop, to see him outside: he was leaning on a metallic green Mercedes Benz Vbooth. 'He is a snub for sure, showing off his car like that.' Every piece of advice she had been given about strangers fell to the ground that day. She was about to cross the road when something touched her feet. She bent down to remove the chocolate wrapper that the wind deposited on her. There was something bright beside her. She slanted her head to see what it was; it was a white fluffy dog, the owner had chained it outside the supermarket.

It was causing a scene so she decided to keep an eye on it. Unfortunately, it wouldn't let her go so he left leaning on the car and joined her in playing with the dog while he told her his well-rehearsed lines.

She found it irritating that he continued clearing his throat, then complained when she could no longer tolerate it. A nurse walking out of the shop noticed his swollen ears and told him to come with her; Athena reluctantly tagged along.

They went into the pharmacy and the nurse spoke to her friend over the counter, who was wrapped up in a novel; she reluctantly closed the novel and quickly scurried away. She returned with a first aid kit and a little black bag with glove in hand. It was later that day that they realised that he was allergic. He was allergic to dogs: her favourite pet!

Her beeping phone broke into her reminiscence but she didn't feel like talking to Nadine. *Oh Moses, what happened? Did I do anything wrong?* She couldn't see Moses the same way, not after what he had just done to her. *If I was to ask for a divorce, what will I say is the reason?* Nadine's mother's words crept in to club her on the head.

She could just about see the woman shaking her head saying, 'divorce is not an option' - the woman was so black and white. She wondered if Nadine's mother would see things differently now, but shook her head and sniggered at the idea.

♥♥♥

Armed with the information Ihinòsé's sources had provided after just one week, she needed to find a student who was ready to relinquish their key card for a day or two.

The willing participant was a final year computing student who had just replaced his key card but insisted on a minimum of £4,000.00 for the 'inconvenience'. The money wasn't as large as she had anticipated, but it was just bad timing. What would be considered her 'home and abroad' was £2,075.00, and by the following day, it would be £1,300.60 after all direct debits were made.

As she sat on the dining table, toying with her food while pondering her next course of action, her phone rang. Her account had been credited with £10,000.00, but wasn't sure she should be glad just yet. Determined to find out where it came from, she browsed her internet banking account. It was from a Mrs. Kolawole.

Who on earth is this? Why would she send money to my account at this critical time, eh? What if I pay this boy, and then it turns out to be an error then the bank will pounce on me with greedy sticky claws. Or did one of Olamide's debtors mistake my account for his? – Their account numbers were similar except for the interchanged last two digits. Before the end of office hours, she had braced herself for whatever came next and withdrew the money.

On seeing the money, the student took her on tour around the university to see where all the notice boards were located. After doing that, he asked her why she needed to know where they were situated. She pretended not to have heard him, and he didn't ask again. He gave her his key card which was to be slipped under his room door when she was through. To save her from sleeping too late she set the alarm for every hour until midnight. She wanted to be there for eleven thirty; by then; the school security must have finished their final rounds.

She ensured she had picked the ones where her husband's face wasn't noticeable from the lot the photographer had sent – feeling a bit paranoid she had collected the SD card he had used. Each time she placed a picture on the notice board, she felt exposed. She felt so exposed that when she got home, she gave herself a good scrub.

Katherine Ferdinand was the President of the Afro-Caribbean Society. She had gone clubbing with her friends to mark her third birthday in the same year. A few members of her team had gotten wind of the news, and tried to get in touch with her but when they failed they decided to take the pictures down themselves. Eleven o'clock in the morning during an exam term was very late; even her clumsy rival had already posted most of the pictures on his *Facebook* page.

Tomorrow is your turn, Crystal Jonas: Crystal Jonas indeed. Cristabel Crentsil Duku, you should cut you coat according to your size my dear. She was glad that she had undertaken to contact Ihinòsé even though what they found relaxing was slightly different. The sleuths she provided were underpaid, unemployed, and bored and were willing to get their hands dirty, but she wasn't ready to get hers dirty.

Eight

The bank was too crowded to identify a bank teller. Athena craned her neck about the same time a brunette bob opened a door and walked into the teller unit and twitched up the blind. Then a voice boomed, 'To teller number four, please.' She didn't get there on time – people had jutted out of their line to queue there. She didn't know how long she could stand while waiting her turn; she was hungry. Her new shoes pinched her toes, and she had a determined urge to pee.

She started tapping her feet and hopping from one foot to the other. The bank didn't have enough space for a toilet. She waited till the crowd had dispersed, but she could no longer hold it in. She dashed out of the bank to a library close by. She just about went in her pants before sitting down on the toilet seat that she would normally clean thoroughly before. She tidied up, and glanced at her wrist; it was exactly 3:17PM. Her stomach growled furiously just as two ladies came into the convenience; she turned slightly red. One of the women smiled weakly, and the other sniggered.

She resisted the urge to enter the restaurant as the smells of food wafted past her; then again she was in a hurry, she walked so briskly that she crashed into someone who fell on two other people. This time she was as red as a tomato; then prepped herself before apologizing profusely.

She sneezed so hard it caused her to feel lightheaded. She leaned on a chair, took a few deep breaths, then started walking to the bank. She wobbled a little and almost fell, but someone guided her. She felt that it was the same person because his perfume made her sneeze again. She was walking haphazardly. The people around thinking she was drunk gave way, allowing her ease to the counter.

An elderly man smiled at her, revealing tobacco-stained teeth. She wasn't watching his hand, but was staring at his teeth until he said, "Go on, we don't have all day." She nodded her thanks.

A minute after her transactions, she was at a pay phone, then the restaurant. Needing a sugar boost, she ordered a chocolate almond ice cream. She couldn't shake off the feeling that someone was following her. She looked around like she was looking for a shop, while scanning the crowd to know for sure that someone was following her and not in her imagination.

She checked her list, rummaged her bag for a piece of paper to rearrange the items but produced a paper in which Nadine had written her address and smiled. She crossed out all of the items she could order online. She looked up to the wall behind her, and saw a WIFI sign. After connecting to the internet, she started making purchases via her phone, but left out the turkey. She wanted to get the turkey in person. She didn't like the yuletide season because of the cooking, and especially because of how she felt about the turkey; no matter how well cooked, it always seemed dry. She relocated to the gazebo when the sun became too warm to bear. Suddenly her view became obscured; she slanted a look to her side, and frowned. The sun was still very high.

She squinted as she raised her head. She couldn't make out who it was until he spoke. She froze, regaining her composure almost immediately; then glided up the chair to sit up.

"How are you?" he repeated also pulling out a chair opposite her. He sat down and stared at her, smiling. He looked like a creepy shadow of himself.

Athena held her bag tightly.

"You look good..." Then he paused before adding, "Aren't you glad to see me?"

She gave him a condescending look.

"I guess I deserve that," he murmured.

She scooped up her glasses and the items she was working with, and made to get up.

He blocked her and set his can of diet coke down on the table. His action along with his cold eyes rattled her. She sat down, mostly because she couldn't feel her legs anymore. He raised his sunglasses and crossed his arms. He appraised her, "Fancy seeing you here." He said, grimly.

She frowned, but said nothing.

"You're bent on not talking to me. That's fine, but I only... I have to apologize for what happened that day..." Athena attempted to get up, but he grabbed her hand firmly. "Please, hear me out! Hear what I have to say, okay?"

A part of her wanted to hear what he had to say so she waited.

"What do I get you?" he asked.

She shook her head.

He shrugged. "I'm sorry about that day, I really am. I needed the money. It was easier for me to be harsh to you than to tell you how I really felt about you. You see, you were one of the poshest girls in college then. I couldn't possibly match up to the calibre of people you hung out with... not counting that big mouthed friend of yours...." He swallowed, frowning. "Everyone thought I was well off, but the truth is that my dad had gambled his way into bankruptcy. He even cleaned out my trust fund, even the money my mum left me, everything! My background is... was... was a lie, and I jumped at every opportunity to make a quick buck to be able to pay my fees."

His voice was so raw with pain that his Australian accent crept up. He was quiet for a few minutes. He raised an eyebrow as well as look eagerly at her; possibly to find out if she bought his story. She had learned that he had used that story for many girls back then, and on one occasion wooed a girl to the extent of going to Las Vegas to do a drive-thru wedding. He moved his hands towards her, but she took her hands off the table, and watched him clench his fist. She froze momentarily with concern. She calmed down when she saw him scratch the nape of his neck. "You understand, yes?"

It was Athena's turn to lean back, and cross her arms. In addition, she wore her glasses, crossed her legs, and curved her lips slightly.

Desmond sighed. "Please give me a chance to do right by you. I know you liked me then, and I can make you like me again. I'll make it up to you, you'll see."

Athena shook her head, and dug a handkerchief out of her bag.

Desmond looked at her leopard print *Jimmy Choo* bag, and licked his lips.

She gave him a look of appraisal; he hadn't shaved in days, and his hair was tousled and rough unlike his usual salt and pepper hairstyle, which he shampooed in the salon every two weeks. His nails were dirty and chapped. He leaned in to pick up his can of Coke, and she saw the inside collar of his shirt. It was lined with dirt. His coat was dishevelled; it looked a size too big. Her conclusion: he was broke, short and simple.

Desmond was dreaming about what he could get from her; she wore a *Versace* dress, a *Burberry* mac, and shoes that were certainly from *Christian Louboutin*, or who else would be audacious with red soles? She also flaunted a *Cartier* tank francaise small model watch – identical to Cindy's own, *Chanel no.5* - he had bought it once for his Nan, Swarovski crystals jewellery, and her glossy blonde hair was tied up in a chignon. He always wondered why she never let it down.

He was searing with excitement when he realised she wasn't wearing a wedding band. *She still has feelings for me or she would have emptied her ice cream on me the way her friend did with her drink. That swan, well she is history I suppose they are no longer friends, probably discovered their differences.* "You're awful quiet!" he sounded a tad impatient.

"Am I?" Athena asked matter-of-factly.

"Please, we can start afresh. I promise I'll be good to you."

Athena sniggered.

"I'll take care of you, as soon as we get married."

"I thought you were married."

"Married? No...Not married, no! Is that why you're hesitating? You know me –"

"I don't know you. I don't even want to know you."

"Come on... you can't mean that? All right, what do I do to prove my love to you?" He laughed nervously, and scratched his head.

"*Desmond*, I'm married!" Athena gave him a smug look.

"That's a laugh, no you're not." He stuttered as he removed his shaking hands from the table.

"Why?" she squinted, wearing a wicked grin.

"You don't have a wedding band."

"Neither do you!"

"But I'm not married. I mean, Marigold and I were very young then and she deceived me, but it's all resolved now."

Athena pulled her chair back, gathering enough space to ease her exit. She gathered her things and bent down to pick up her phone that had fallen.

"Oh really, resolved yeah, resolved yeah. You, you."

Athena looked round upon hearing this. She watched a heavily pregnant woman's glass of water tip over Desmond's head. She started laughing and the woman glared at her; so she raised her hand in surrender and left, but not before dropping a few things in the bin. She could hear their bickering behind her, but she didn't care. She was glad that she didn't feel anything for him.

Meanwhile, Desmond had seen her drop things in the bin, and swiftly went to it before anyone could dunk their mess. There was an address on one of the papers. The pregnant woman was still chin-wagging behind him.

As the weeks progressed, Desmond sent her roses, lily of the valley, glorosia, lisianthus, chocolates, and cards so much so that her husband was sure she was seeing someone; they'd been so out of touch that he didn't remember that her all-time favourites were hydrangea and red carnations. She also didn't like chocolate unless it was in ice cream. She couldn't help wondering where Desmond could have gotten the money to buy the things he sent as he was obviously broke.

"Who is Desmond?" Moses asked.

"Sorry?" she asked, not looking up as she dug out a nail buffer.

"Who is Desmond?" he repeated.

"No one." She hissed and started to buffer her nails.

"I'm talking to you, Athena!"

She looked up at him and said, "Wow! You can actually call me by name. It must be serious!" she mocked and went back to buffering her toenails.

She saw him walk menacingly towards her; and her thought flashed back to her resolve on the staircase in 2003, after Desmond pawned her in order to win a bet; then she recalled how Moses tore her clothes then something snapped that made her well with anger, so that when he raised his hand to strike her, she skilfully dodged it and instinctively picked up the large paper weight at the same time.

He turned her to face him with force that the paper weight in her hand rammed into his temple. Before she could react, he was on the floor: her eyes were closed at the time. When she opened them to see her husband on the floor, she froze.

She shook him vigorously, no response. She knelt beside him, shaking and wishing it was a dream. Hysterically, she pinched herself twice before she confirmed that it was real.

She wanted to call of the police, hesitated and called for an ambulance instead. She was still holding on to the paper weight when the knock on the door brought her back to reality. Startled, she dropped the paper weight which landed on her feet. She squealed, afraid of the alarm screaming might cause, and subsequently limped to the door. She welcomed the team with a placid smile; trying to ignore her pain and ultimately trying to hide it.

They stood in the hallway waiting for her, but she just stared at them. She was lost in thought for a minute. She didn't want them to see her limp so she pointed in the direction of the sitting room. The quirky male nurse raised his brow while the female nurse eyed Athena suspiciously; she probably thought it was a prank.

"My husband is in there!" she shouted, sounding hysterical.

They shrugged and went ahead of her. She followed them. She yelped after accidentally hitting her injured foot on the door.

"So what happened?" the nurse asked.

"Happened, what happened?" Athena asked, feigning innocence while trying to ignore the pain that was coursing through her veins from her feet.

The female nurse arched her brow, looking at Athena intently.

"Do I look all right?" Athena said, suddenly. "My husband is lying in there. He's not moving."

"Ma'am, you need to calm down," the other nurse said.

A few minutes later, while they were checking his vitals, Moses opened his eyes. Squinting, he surveyed his environment.

"How are you feeling?" the female nurse asked.

Moses looked at her for a few seconds. He glanced around the room, and then at his wife, who now had an ice pack on her feet and blinked.

"How do you feel?"

Moses said nothing, just stared at Athena. She gave him a wicked smile. Suffice it to say, he never raised his hand towards her again.

Nine

Bettina was meticulous. She had a timetable for everything; from baking, knitting, crocheting, sewing, embroidering, visiting of friends, going to the park, and making phone calls.

Temitope didn't like doing anything that would give her the excuse to remain in one place for long hours, except if it was to watch movies. She was bored to death of staying at home, coupled with the fact that her daughters were now living at school. That was a choice she hated, but had to take because they were getting too dependent on her. So, when Athena invited her, she welcomed it with open arms. Temitope loved being at Bettina's; neither of the women were the type of people to pry into other people's affairs plus Bettina made mouth-watering dishes that she couldn't resist taking home.

It had been over a week since they'd visited the park; Bettina didn't feel like going anywhere. Bettina's son, Clinton opened the door. He no longer looked emaciated. "Good morning, come on in," he said.

"Hello!" Athena and Temitope sighed simultaneously.

"Hi! Welcome. Tea?"

Both women regarded each other, and chorused, "Coffee!"

He came back a few minutes later, "You both sounded exhausted! Are you all right?"

"Yes, we are." Athena collected her cup of coffee. "Thank you!"

Temitope nodded her thanks, and took a sip. "What about Bettina? Is she stuck in traffic?"

"She is upstairs; I'll go and get her."

"Is she all right?" Athena asked.

"Well... about that" Clinton started.

"That will be enough, son." Bettina said.

"Good morning," the other women said.

"Good morning, Mummy!" Clinton said, walking over to his mother. He hugged her, picked up his jacket, and went out.

Temitope gave Athena a slanted querying look from just above the rim of her cup.

Athena shrugged.

"Your body language speaks volumes." Bettina settled down opposite them.

"We're just curious..." Athena started.

"Yes, you've not been yourself lately. For instance, you used to force us to go to the park for picnics and now you -"

"Temitope! That's enough."

"I see..." Bettina said solemnly, nodding.

"Is it about your daughter?" Athena's voice was laced with concern.

"Daughter?" Temitope almost spilled her coffee.

"Yes daughter, what's with you?" Athena whispered, nudging her friend.

"You have two children?" Temitope asked Bettina.

"Yes, two, my children; my daughter Ibukun..."

"A boy and a girl, see? Complete. I still need.... even if it's just one." Athena sighed.

"Don't sound like that." Bettina sounded sympathetic.

Bettina fingered her necklace, lost in thought. Then she shook her head, and sighed. "We had a row; it was the worst, and obviously the last straw for her, because I woke up to an empty house the following day.

At that time, Clinton was still in boarding school. She took everything that belong to her, the pictures.... and left. All I have to remember her by ..." She unhooked the cultured pearl necklace, laid it gently on her thighs, and began to stroke the beads before breaking down in tears.

She fought it back, almost choking as she gulped. "Now I look back and I wonder what we were really fighting about? I honestly don't remember." She wiped her face and twisted her face and clasped the necklace back in place. "I should have been her mother." She whispered, her face filled with anguish, and she started crying again. This time, no one could console her.

After a while, she closed her eyes, humming and smiling.

Athena and Temitope looked at each other, confused. None had the courage to ask any questions.

Athena exhaled loudly. "I have to go. Thanks Bettina!" She hugged her friends. "And you..." she pointed at Temitope. "You're a troublemaker."

"That's my cue." Temitope quickly blew a kiss at Bettina, then walked briskly to the dining room to carry her bag and slip away.

That night, neither Temitope nor Athena could sleep. They pondered on Bettina's words, not sure of what they were to make of it. As they began to drift off, they realised that it was the part about not knowing what the fight was about that ate at them.

♥♥♥

Three days after the fourth week of classes, Bettina told her students that she was going to Northumbria for a few days to take care of her niece who was recovering from a major surgery. Athena needed a distraction, especially now that she had become acutely aware of someone following her. It had been going on for the past three weeks - but then it could be her emotions playing tricks on her which were more frequent than the change of chords in Beethoven's *Hallelujah.*

Athena saw it as an opportunity to give Bettina's house a makeover. She gave the house a look of appraisal, making a mental note to recycle some of Bettina's things. She would get the rest from a charity shop first before going to any other outlay.

She roped Temitope in, and they enlisted the help of Clinton. On the day Bettina left, Clinton got the planning permission for a few structural changes to the house. That same day he found a carpenter to agree to fix the steps the following day.

They arrived simultaneously.

Athena had already bought coveralls for each of them. Temitope brought a camera, a camcorder, and a large football shaped cake. Athena felt like a domestic goddess in navy blue coveralls, which accentuated her blue eyes. They started cleaning from the back of the house to avoid interruptions by Bettina's intrusively amiable neighbours.

By the time they had emptied the garden and the rooms upstairs, Clinton was tired. He had to leave the rest of the work to the women and the building team. Athena made a mental note to ask him what was wrong with him when there was more privacy.

The following day, Athena juggled between painting the kitchen wall and keeping Temitope away from one of the painters; he was already purple with nervous laughter, and looked like he was less than eighteen. The builders had worked through the night, dropping the kitchen floor down by sixteen inches to make it the same level as the rest of the house. Clinton had chosen black laminate for the kitchen floor to create a demarcation for the kitchen area.

The carpenters had moved the arch to the back of the house. This they did, extending the porch to include a sun deck. The hollow wood which was used to create a zone between the kitchen and the sitting room was removed to create enough space for a six-sitter dining room and the hallway was halved.

The space was required because Bettina was like a mother to all in the neighbourhood. Her being away didn't seem to deter people from stopping by, peering through the spaces they had boarded up, or peering over her shoulders any time she answered the door.

The kitchen wall was white, and the multifunctional wooden cabinet in modern curves was glossy in teal, and topped off with a graphite work top. Temitope's phone rang while she was applying varnish on the dining table. As she walked away to answer the call, Athena remembered her phone. Olamide had left her a few messages.

She was so preoccupied with the homework Bettina had been giving her that she didn't realise that it had been weeks since she last saw him. Thinking of him made her wonder if she wanted to go back to the room they had once shared. She shook her head, unfolded the chairs and placed them around the dining table.

The visitor's room downstairs was converted to a study to provide the industrious children a place of their own. She opened the boxes of children's books she had bought from *Oxfam* and *British Heart Foundation*, and realised she hadn't bought any encyclopaedias – not that it mattered. The room was painted white. The shelves were in glossy caramel. The bean bags were in orange, brown and navy blue while the floor was covered in a red, blue, black, beige, yellow, and green striped carpet. The hallway was in magnolia with the floors in the same colour as the kitchen.

The plush blood-red leather three-sitter settee was flanked by two sofas in stone, and the third in beige to match the thick navy blue rug. The silver box TV, which had no more buttons and wouldn't come on unless it was smacked several times, was taken upstairs under Clinton's orders. It was replaced with a 72 inch flat screen TV, placed on Beech wood shelves. It had replaced the white ones that held the other TV. The pictures that were on the fireplace were scattered around it. There was a sculpture that flowed endlessly; the bottom looked like boiling water, and there was a space underneath and in between the glass and wood design; Athena eyed it with jealousy, wishing it was hers. The fireplace was painted in three tone colours of bronze, charcoal-grey, and brown.

♥♥♥

It was already four in the morning by the time they had finished. Athena looked at the finished work feeling like she had just hit a jackpot. In a subtle way, it reminded her of when she got three scholarships in a row; not that she needed the scholarships at the time. She wanted to prove that she didn't need her mother's money or lifestyle to succeed. It was a good thing though, because at the same time, her mother lost everything to husband number three.

Corazon, you're the most ridiculous of mothers, but I miss you! Cora was oblivious to everything else except her plastic surgeon. She then remarried husband number two on a cruise, but divorced him in the same month. A week after her divorce, she became a mistress to a member of the imperial family who gave her any precious stone she needed.

Nadine's mother however was her role model and her strength. She couldn't help the hunger for her mother's approval, and continued to itch for her mother's affection until she died. No matter how hard Nadine's mother tried to be there for her, that void was never filled.

But now, as she watched her creation come to life, she felt both relief and the urge to do more. It was what she studied, but never felt like taking it up. Maybe after her classes with Bettina, she would go for it fulltime.

It was too early to order pizza so they settled for sharing dry toast with canned Coke for her and Temitope while the rest settled for a cider. Knowing that Bettina wouldn't take kindly to the changes they had made behind her back, they employed Clinton to play decoy. They also invited all of the children in the neighbourhood to come over on Monday. It was a bank holiday, and the day Bettina was to arrive.

Ten

Bettina wasn't just happy with the changes. She was thrilled; pleased that her house had a facelift and that her husband's things weren't tossed out. She was also certain that they had too much time on their hands and gave them more work to do.

Moses had left Athena a note by the time she got home last night. She didn't read it but then he started calling, and he called all day. By evening, he had called four times, and by the fifth time Bettina insisted that she answer it. He was asking for permission to come back home.

"What? It's your house, isn't it?" She asked. Then she punched the phone.

Bettina had noticed that the needlework classes were Athena and Temitope's excuse to stay out of their homes and practically enforced them to make their marriages work and not let another woman do that for them. It was a month later that Annette started talking to Moses, but their conversations were monosyllabic.

Bettina always prepared lunch for the two of them. They had a special one on Fridays which Temitope always eloped with. This time Bettina made them chicken soba noodles which smelt heavenly, but Athena picked at her food. Temitope took Annette's bowl without asking her and emptied it into her own. Athena wasn't surprised; she was more concerned with her dinner date with her husband and anytime she thought of it, she felt the urge to puke.

"Are you okay?" Bettina asked her.

"I have been feeling a little off lately." Athena drank a glass of water.

"Let's go to Peckham," Temitope said.

"Why?" Athena asked.

She lowered her head and said, "I want you to come with me to see a spiritualist."

Athena gave her a slanted look.

"She will do no such thing!" Bettina dragged a bale of yarn with her.

"I don't believe in such things." Athena helped Bettina divide the yarn amongst them. "Why would you suggest that anyway?"

"Does it matter?" Bettina sighed as she pulled a chair.

Athena shrugged.

"Don't take her to such places, you hear me?"

"Yes ma, but –"

"No but.... I'm really serious o." Bettina groaned, loudly.

"Okay, okay!" Temitope whispered, startled by Bettina's outburst.

"Bettina, are you okay?" Athena sounded concerned.

"Yes, it's all this talk about spiritualist, herbalist etcetera."

Athena and Temitope frowned.

"It was only a suggestion." Temitope sulked.

"You never told me why you suggested it."

"Well...isn't it obvious? You do want children, don't you?"

"I do want children."

"From your mouth to God's ears!" Bettina touched her mouth and raised her hands up.

"But I'll not go down that road." Athena completed her sentence.

"You need a solution –"

"Are you trying to freak me out? Because this goes way beyond trying to annoy me." Athena asked while Bettina gave Temitope a warning look.

Temitope shrugged.

"I need to go now before the shops close."

"Why?" Temitope looked up.

"I need to get something to wear."

"Come on, it's only a dinner with your husband." Temitope made a hissing sound as she cleaned her teeth with her tongue.

Athena glared at Temitope.

"Don't mind your friend. But always remember, God is your strength!"

"Fine. What about your neighbour?" Temitope asked.

"What about my neighbour?" Athena asked, absentmindedly.

"She is an addict who leaves her children behind for days on end without taking care of them."

"Oh dear!" Athena looked at her friend, suspiciously. "How did you know that?"

"I have my ways. Besides, I hate being bored." Temitope responded.

Bettina slapped the back of Temitope's head lightly. "It's a way of opening your womb so you'll become fertile."

Temitope nodded in agreement, rubbing her head.

Athena slapped Temitope's hand off her bowl of rice pudding. "That's not humanly possible and F.Y.I., I am fertile."

"Aha!" Bettina opened the fridge to replace the tin of evaporated milk. "Humanly possible you say, but God works in mysterious ways."

"Every good deed gets a reward," Temitope dunked her spoon in Athena's pudding.

Athena looked down, with her shoulders slumped with exhaustion and her emotions sapped. She had resolved not to argue with her friends, especially Temitope, who didn't know how and when to shut her mouth. She used to tolerate her because she couldn't bear to be alone, but now she was just the needed distraction from her emotional debility.

"What is it?" Bettina placed her hands on her shoulder.

Athena shook her head, shrugging.

"You give alms don't you?" Temitope asked.

"So, what is wrong with that?" Athena asked

"Why?" Temitopc asked, taking away Athena's dish. "Why do you give alms?"

"Because I can afford to," Athena replied.

"Oh! Anyway... then why don't you just help the woman, I mean your neighbour."

"Because I can't afford to." Athena retorted, now losing her appetite.

"Why?" the other two women exclaimed, at once.

Athena cleaned her hands, "I don't want to get attached and find it difficult to let go. The way I feel, I may take drastic measures, maybe ask her to let me have them. You know adopt them, but Moses..." Athena sighed.

"Oh my God!" Bettina and Temitope exclaimed.

Bettina appeared to be amused and Temitope laughed excitedly.

"Oh yes! I thought of that. Look, you've got two children between you two. I don't have any and because of that, that hypocrite of a woman can talk back at me. Luckily for her, and unfortunately for me, she is my mother-in-law." She sighed deeply, "I'm not getting any younger and IVFs are expensive."

"But you can afford it!" Bettina took more dishes to the sink.

"I've used it twice; I can no longer afford the stress and tension that comes with it. Besides that woman is breathing down my neck. I fit break her neck!" Athena clenched her fists.

Bettina and Temitope looked at each other, trying to stifle their laughter.

"Wow! You're sounding very Nigerian," Temitope said. Bettina nudged her, giving her a warning look.

"Am I?" she smiled. "I guess I needed to vent a little."

"Good for you!" Temitope said.

Bettina nodding in agreement.

"Well..." Bettina stood up. "Don't you have dinner with your husband?"

"I suddenly don't feel like going." She said, feigning tiredness.

"You don't have to," Temitope said.

"Oh shut up! And you, don't listen to her."

Temitope licked the last of the pudding off the spoon. "I haven't seen your friend in a while."

"You mean Nadine. She has been in France a long time now but she will be visiting next month. It seems like only yesterday since Nadine said that and years since I saw her."

"Well, I do have to tell you, she gives me headaches." Temitope licked her fingers.

"Really? Well I do have to tell you too, she said the same thing about you." Athena said.

Eleven

"Where are you?" Temitope asked.

"I'm at home." Athena deftly caught the bowl of popcorn that was about to be toppled from her lap, then switched the phone to speaker mode.

"You are sure? Because I just saw you and your husband go into a restaurant."

"I'm pretty sure you've come up with another excuse for gossip." Athena responded in between throwing popcorn into her mouth.

"My dear, I know your husband's car and I know your husband doesn't conduct business meetings at that particular restaurant okay!"

"How do you know where they conduct their meetings?"

"Never mind. So?"

"'So' what?"

"Well, I said I just saw your husband at the restaurant."

"Which one is it?" Athena asked, reluctant to listen.

"Remember the one I showed you on the high street, the Indian tandoori one, yes?"

"Okay! Whatever you say! Can I get off now?" Athena said.

"Okay o! Tomorrow when something happens, don't say I didn't tell you o! Hmm!"

As soon as the phone call ended, Athena dialled her husband's phone number, it was switched off but she didn't want to leave a message. Athena's face turned red with anger, the movie was no longer interesting enough to distract her; she didn't even remember that she had a bowl of popcorn on her thighs when she got up, and she stomped out of the sitting room straight to the guest room. She called his number again and again and for the next hour she paced around the room throwing thing around. She paused, thrust her hand through her hair and tugged it.

I need to think! I need to think! I need to clear my head! She started pacing again, this time more fervently, crossing and uncrossing her arms with each turn.

After a while, she plopped on the chair and sat upright looking like someone in a trance, then she suddenly got up and walked to the window. She opened the curtain and leaned on the sill as she looked at the rainbow and smiled weakly. She turned towards the toilet when she felt the urge to puke, then went back to the sitting room.

She took her phone, captured the rainbow perfectly and then packed her things from the guest room back to her bedroom. After exercising, she took a long soak, then called the restaurant to speak to a girl she helped get a job there, ordered the same food her husband ate and went into her walk-in closet, coming out twenty minutes later with a two-in-one grey sequin dress.

Her phone stopped ringing just before she picked it up. She saw four missed calls and called the numbers; not knowing who the callers were, she decided to dial the number. It was from both Nadine and Temitope and they were coming with their spouses for dinner – she was now used to impromptu guest.

Athena looked at her clothes and decided to change into something different for when the guests would arrive, but not before making another call to the Indian restaurant.

After an hour of going through garbs she settled for a royal blue lace knee-length dress with three-quarter sleeves. She wore a gold south sea pearl necklace, her late mother's most priced jewellery which was the only existing property her mother left her, then she strapped on the watch Moses gave her on her birthday.

She wiped down the first makeup and started all over to wear colours that would accentuate her deep blue, almond shaped eyes, and she decided to wear the *Maybelline* lipstick because of its name; *pleasure me red.* She looked at her face from side to side, slapped her face lightly and pinched her cheeks, before letting her hair down and then used the curler on it to make it bounce. Temitope called again while she was setting the table.

They arrived almost simultaneously and she invited them in and was alarmed when Nadine nearly knocked her down. She was pregnant, very pregnant. *Wow! Any minute now she will have a baby.* It was like someone left a hammer to fall on her head; she sniffed and blinked as she tried to hide her pain. She held her chest trying to breath; it felt like life was being drained out of her and she could do nothing about it. *I guess being fertile is not dependant on being a decent girl.*

As soon as everyone was out of earshot, Temitope went back to meet Athena who was leaning on the door and sobbing. She cautioned Athena and pushed her into the washroom. A few minutes later, Athena went to answer the door. Moses was at the door and a lady stood behind him. She couldn't help wondering why the lady behind him looked like she had just seen a ghost but shrugged it off.

"Ehen...Cindy," Temitope beckoned Cindy and pulled a chair out patting it, then turned to Moses "Thanks for giving her a lift." Cindy lowered her head and rolled her eyes.

Noticing this, Athena's suspicion dissipated and she joined hands with them and prayed. With one look at her husband, the irritation ended. He was obviously uncomfortable and she enjoyed his uneasiness. Moses gave his wife a slanted look, frowning; *she has never let hair down before and it was always straight. What is she up to?* There was a feeling she couldn't quite shake off as she looked over at Cindy.

Moses couldn't take his eyes off his wife, especially when he noticed that the food on the table was the same thing he had eaten earlier; he got up to use the toilet. When he got up his legs shook involuntarily. After dinner he insisted on helping her take the dishes to the kitchen. He asked suggestive questions to find out if she knew he was at the same restaurant she ordered food from.

He helped her replace some items in the cupboard. He let a plate drop and break, but she was oblivious to his grimace. Then he wrapped his arms around her tightly and started kissing her neck as he snuggled her closely, but she was rigid. Athena didn't want it to stop and at the same time she didn't want to forget what he had done to her. Someone cleared their throat behind them and she couldn't help guessing who it was. She was both annoyed and relieved.

"I'm sorry, Temi said to tell you someone's on the phone." Cindy said, staring daggers at Athena who ignored her and cradled the phone, but the caller ID wasn't clear. Then it rang again.

"Hello...really...that's good news. Oh that's perfect! I'll let him know right away!" she covered the mouthpiece and said, "Honey!" Her voice trailed off when she discovered that he was no longer there and the desserts were still on the counter.

She shrugged, placed the desserts on a platter and took them to the sitting room; she found it odd that the dining was dark while the guests were still in the house. She noticed Moses and Cindy were missing but wasn't interested. She went back into the kitchen through the hallway and walked towards the dining. The sound of avid moaning of jolly recreation was unmistakeable and by all means causing her grief.

She leaned against the wall, torn between going ahead to catch them in the act, tearing them apart or letting it go on because they had guests, opting to spare her thoughts of the picture imprint she sneaked back before their guest would realize their host and hostess were absent, her right shoe got stuck in something.

She bent down to pull it, then recoiled as if she had just touched a naked wire and walked briskly to the sitting room, half running and half walking. She shuddered as she sat down with the others as they watched a pirated movie while having dessert. Moses was back in his seat so she concluded that the girl was pleasuring herself until she noticed that Olamide was absent. She ruled it out because Temitope would have known; as if on cue Temitope looked around and frowned.

"Where is my husband?" Temitope asked.

"Oh! He said he had to get back to the office to pick something up."

"And Cindy?"

"Maybe she followed him; after all she's his PA."

Athena frowned. Moses got up and said, "May I be excused."

"Really, now?" Athena said, staring at him.

"I'm going to fax some documents. Would you like to come with?"

She turned to face the television.

Moses bent down to whisper, "Tobias just came in. He'll only crash this night."

Maybe I imagined the sound of lovemaking. I definitely heard it, maybe Tobias smuggled a woman in. I best make sure. She got up to make sure but Nadine pulled her back down with a tight grip. She gave Nadine a querying look. Nadine pointed down as if she was making an invisible moss code.

Athena looked down and found nothing and gave her friend a stern look. Nadine shook her head and beckoned her husband in a voice that sounding like a baby whimpering. She continued to stare at her friend now confused, to worsen it Olamide came in but she didn't hear the clicking sound of the doorknob.

Nadine started clicking her fingers which everyone thought was a reaction to the movie. Everyone became uncomfortable when she started moaning and raising her voice and gasping at her husband. It wasn't until Temitope jumped up as something cold smeared her buttocks that Nadine's husband paused the movie and turned to his wife.

"My water don break o!" Nadine gasped.

"What do you mean? What water?" Athena asked confused as she stretched her hand towards her friend.

Temitope dropped her plate and gave her husband their car keys.

Whose car did Mr. Ademinokan go with then? Where is Moses or that girl?

"We are going to the hospital" Temitope whispered to Athena breaking her from her thought.

"Well, what are you waiting for? Take me to the hospital!" Nadine finally shouted at her husband.

The women were already at the door. Athena stopped abruptly and ran up the stairs, carried the house keys, locked all of the doors. When she got downstairs, she quickly and quietly crept towards the kitchen and picked everything she could lay her hands on from the floor. Then stopped shortly at the guestroom, threw the items in there and locked the door. She sighed, composed herself and then threw the bunch of keys into her purse and left with them: forgetting to lock the front door.

By the time they arrived at the hospital. Cindy was wearing something different and Moses didn't have time to diverse his plan of going through the other exit door and coming in from another wing of the hospital. He nearly jumped out of his skin when he saw it was Temitope at the lobby. He looked for his wife and was a little relieved, *I can deny it!* He quickly went to look for his wife before Temitope had the time to relay whatever she thought she saw.

"Where were you?" Temitope asked Cindy before she had a chance to sit down. Her tone made others sitting around them turn to look at her. "What!" Temitope said when they didn't turn away before turning her attention back to Cindy. "Ehen, I asked you a question."

Cindy sighed and didn't say anything.

"Are you sleeping with Moses? How did you even meet him?"

"What? Why? When? What sort of question is that?"

"Oooh! That's how you want to play it *abi?*"

"Look, I don't know what you are trying to – "

"Hey! Look here," Temitope said with arms akimbo.

Cindy tilted her head back.

"He will never leave his wife for you so I'll advise you to stop whatever you are doing now." Temitope hissed and turned bumping into her husband who was just coming back from the toilet.

"Are you all right?" Olamide asked Temitope who looked him head to toe.

"Yes I am. Excuse me!" She hissed and brushed pass him.

"Where were you?" Olamide asked in a loud whisper as soon as his wife was out of the way.

"Don't raise your voice at me," Cindy warned.

"Where are you coming from?" he asked, ignoring her.

"It's none of your business."

"You're my wife, therefore it is."

Cindy sniggered.

"We had an agreement and you'll be wise to stick to it."

"If you ever threaten me –"

"What will you do?" Olamide sniggered.

"How about telling your wife right now?" Cindy said with a victorious smile.

"I dare you!" he said, sounding a bit cynical as he called her bluff. His heart was already in his mouth but he was determined to put her in her place.

She started sulking then asked, "You think you're in naija, *abi*?" Before making an attempt to leave but he grabbed her arm roughly.

"Don't do what you'll regret especially since you have nothing I really need." He said and let her go.

Athena came back into the waiting room with Moses. She suspected he was up to something because he kept hanging around her. Her eyes fell on a white purse lined with a pink and white flowers and a blue and a green little bird in flight embroidery in Cindy's hand and wondered why she couldn't remember the last place she had seen it.

Temitope came in from the opposite side of the hospital with Nadine's husband. A few minutes later the doctor asked Nadine's husband to join her and then he came back an hour later with a very broad smiling like he was advertising a tooth paste. They all got up to join him in going to see his daughter at the nursery. Cindy also stood up to join them.

"You can go now." Temitope said grimly, standing in Cindy's way and Athena was glad.

"Why?" Cindy and Olamide asked.

"Why?" Temitope asked her husband and he raised his hand in surrender. "You have got work tomorrow and you've had a really long day, so go on, go and rest eh! Goodnight!"

Cindy looked at Olamide, who turned away immediately and rushed to meet the others who were already staring gooey-eyed at the babies through the glass. Moses' back was turned to Cindy the whole time. Cindy was shocked, they had just made out in his house and she felt it was a sign that he had made up his mind about divorcing his wife to be with her. She left fuming and promised to deal with both of them.

There were so many rows of white beds except for the creamy pink heads and occasional ebony heads. As if Nadine's baby knew she was being pointed at she started crying and most of the babies join in crescendo.

♥♥♥

Athena watched the babies as they reminded her of cherubs but without the wings and bit her lips to hold back her tears. Moses held her close, making her lean on him. *I'm going to have my own kids Moses, you'll see, I'll carry my own children too.*

Twelve

It was always easier if there was no trace, no evidence of it. She gave a scornful laugh; three miscarriages was evidence. She hadn't held onto a pregnancy since then. She closed the book and got up, knocking her knee on the half open drawer. She nursed her knee as she slipped her feet into her slippers. She went to the garage to clean it up. While she was at it, she came across old photographs she hadn't seen in years. She sat down on a fireproof box, and started perusing them. She flipped through some pictures of when they started dating - he was her first boyfriend.

He looked delicate then in his lanky form. She smiled when she realised how handsome he now is. She wasn't looking half bad either, except for the fact that she looked taller then. *I was thin that's why!* She sniggered when she got to her mother-in-law's pictures; there seemed to be many of them, especially at the christening of her brother-in-law's daughter. *Trust her to be in my face all of the time.* Then she held onto one of them as memories washed over her.

It was a cold misty morning in the December of 1997; she had sneaked out of Olamide's house and was about to get into her house, but her annoying younger sister had locked their bedroom window which meant her father would come back from work and all hell would be let loose.

Each time she twisted her wrist to check the time, she would look over the fence which was just over three inches taller; she started banging on the window with her shoes when she realised that her father would be back in ten minutes, but her sister still didn't respond. Two minutes before her father was due back, her mother opened the window, and let her in.

The excitement that she experienced before her father got home was short-lived. Her father went out for an age group meeting and left within the hour. Glad to have escaped her father's wrath, she turned around to see her mother at the door holding a cane.

Her mother had two rules; one, she must flog you on your buttocks while you lie flat on the ground and two, if you made her miss, she would start the countdown all over. She didn't step out for days, but as soon as she was healed, she ran after Olamide at their meeting place - the back of the palm wine tapper's house.

She had to travel to Oshogbo which was almost a work day's journey because cars did not ply the routes she took. She couldn't risk doing the pregnancy test in Iwo because her father's friend owned the lab there. When the result came out, she felt like someone had poured cold water from the fridge over her. She was in her final year in university, and was in the middle of her school project.

More so, she was afraid of having an abortion, and she had only agreed with Olamide so that he could give her money. To her wildest surprise, he gave her ₦50, 000; this was a guy who never gave her more than ₦500 and that was only twice! The following week as she was brushing her teeth at the back of the house, her mother came out and stood behind her with arms folded. Temitope started taking her bath at the back of the house so that no one would see or hear her hurl her stomach's content.

Her father gave her the research money she requested. As soon as her mother left for a traditional marriage, she carried her already packed bags and a few things she had bought that morning and fortified with ₦67, 216.00, a duffel bag and a battered brown suitcase with black piping, she went to the park to make a journey to her father's grandmother's place - it was the only place she could go where she could be sure she wouldn't be chased away.

Her great-grandmother died a month after she had given birth, and she was practically forced to move in with Iya-gbeji – a name given to a mother of twins - her grandmother whose only motive was to squeeze out whatever money she had left. Fortunately, her great-grandmother had bought her all she needed for the baby, to last for a whole year, and had gone as far as sewing a second layer to the bottom of Temitope's bag to hide the money she came with.

A few months later, on a chilly morning, Temitope came out of Iya-gbeji's house in wee hours of the morning to take her bath before the twins would be awake. It was quite chilly so she decided she was going to get the babies' bath things inside before taking her own bath. She had just finished doing that, and was taking her aluminium bucket of hot water when something, a figure, frightened her. The shrill sound woke almost everyone in the compound up: it was her mother.

Temitope ran into her mother's arms, and was twirled around at least five times before her mother was satisfied that her daughter was all right. Her mother thanked Iya-gbeji but not before raining abuses on the woman and her household for trying to steal her daughter and grandchild from right under her nose just because she didn't give them a son – Temitope's mother was known for her notoriety, and most people stayed away from her, except some who adored her indifference to tradition.

"Mummy, I have two.... "

"To what?" her mother asked, doting on Temitope and pushing her onto a stool made from a cross section of a tree's trunk.

"Two. Mummy, I mean two children." Temitope said.

She was amused at her mother's loss of words and wide eyes and open mouth.

"Eh? Twins…" She danced and eulogized her daughter.

"How did you even know…" Temitope hesitated and continued, "…that I was pregnant?"

"I didn't."

"Then how…"

"Your father. He noticed that you had the same symptoms I had when I was pregnant with you." She said smiling with pride.

"He did?" Temitope asked, astounded.

Her mother nodded, smiling.

"Do you want to see them?"

"Of course, but not now! Let them sleep."

"Oh Mummy, I'm so sorry." Temitope said and laid her head on her mother's lap, "I didn't think you'd approve."

Her mother patted her tenderly, "I don't approve of how you got pregnant, but I'll never reject your child. Children are blessings from God, you know."

"Oh, mummy…"

"Don't be….I wanted more children, and I couldn't give your father anymore; so when he mentioned it, I decided that we would wait until you came to us. When you ran away; I assumed you were afraid."

"Ah! Mummy, I was, oh! You would have killed me."

"Ah! But that would have been after you had given birth, but then when my eyes would fall on the baby, babies, I would find it hard to beat you, so I'll give you a little punishment."

"Mummy please oh! Tamper justice with mercy…" she paused tapping her index finger on her lower lip, "…or is it mercy with justice?"

"Who cares?"

"So..."

"We are taking you back home..." She paused and turned to face her daughter, "...how did you manage without money? How will you cope with the exams you've missed?"

"I didn't miss my exams –"

One of the babies started crying.

Getting up, Temitope said, "Mummy, we have all of the time in the world."

"I'll help you pack your things. Then, I'll go to the park to hire a vehicle that will take us back."

"Back where?"

"Home of course, back to Ibadan."

♥♥♥

She missed her mum now more than ever.

The winter sun was so warm on her face that she stood in front of the garage, lifted her face, closed her eyes and inhaled the cool breeze.

Ever since she set her eyes on the baby pictures in the parenting book, she had not been her best. She wondered what would have happened if she had told her husband about that pregnancy. Maybe she should have kept it, and then not told him who the father was, but knowing the kind of person she was, it would not be long before the words would start reeling out of her mouth then he would kill her for sleeping with his best friend she didn't know.

Thirteen

Temitope's daughters were just four months, a week, and two days old when she joined the January batch of Youth Corps to be of service to Nigeria; even though she didn't go to her primary posting. Unable to cope with missing them, she went home during the weekend every fortnight.

A year later, in 1999 she got a job with a multinational company and six months later she got a new boss: Olamide. They rekindled their relationship almost immediately, mostly because she wanted to have more money - her father had died leaving her mother with a two-day old baby. Olamide's mother did not approve, especially not when she and the governor's wife had a common understanding about the union of their children. Temitope would only be an impediment to that plan.

Temitope, on the other hand, had cleaned up nicely; she bought a two plot land and had started building a permanent residence for her mother and siblings in Ikorodu.

In January she sent Abimbola, her younger sister to Harvard University for a three weeks course. Anderson, her step brother – adopted during her youth service at the age of ten – she sent to the same Navy boarding school that her father attended. She sent her mother to the Maldives for a month. She also made it her primary assignment to make Olamide's mother's life uncomfortable, even if it would hurt her own relationship with Olamide.

Temitope went to meet Olamide in their new rendezvous. She was already in the house when she heard his mother's voice, and hid behind the open door of Olamide's room. His mother was supposed to be in Italy for at least two weeks for two entrepreneurial conventions and a time management workshop.

Then Temitope overheard James, Olamide's elder brother; he was very bad at keeping secrets because he didn't know how to whisper in his raspy, deep bass voice. He shared ownership of a hospital with his wife. Temitope smiled: she had just discovered that James' wife owned seventy percent of it, and was considering taking matters into her hands by looking for a man to impregnate her.

Why wouldn't she after six IVFs? Temitope thought.

James's fear was that she would divorce him. His mother said there was nothing wrong with it; all he had to do was catch her in the act, and ask for a divorce. He told her that they had a pre-nuptial; he would get nothing in a divorce settlement, excluding his share of the hospital.

Temitope had been hiding behind the door for only three minutes and was already restless. She was trying to balance her weight on one foot, then switched to the other when her eyes fell on some papers that were laid out on the bed; curiosity got the best of her. While she was still rifling through them Olamide's mother walked in on her.

She hissed and walked to the bed, "What are you doing here?"

Temitope made a show of going through the papers.

Mrs. Ademinokan quickly bent over the papers, holding them close to her chest, "You didn't answer my question."

Temitope wore a wicked grin, and sized her.

"What do you want?"

Fifteen minutes later they came to an unusual concord; Mrs. Ademinokan was not to object to her son marrying a 'baseless' girl. Olamide noticed his mother's change of attitude towards Temitope but never asked especially as Temitope had made sure their wedding was attended strictly by family and close friends only.

Temitope didn't see the sun go down. She was brought back to reality by Faze's song: a ringtone she used for her private investigators recommended by Ihinòsé. He informed her of a new contender to her marital throne. He wasn't sure the girl in question was an adult by law, and kept insisting that she couldn't be more than fifteen. Olamide had started coming home later than he used to - something he had never done before.

She quickly gulped the remaining liquid from the bottle of *Guinness* stout. She didn't know if she should be proud or feel creepy that he chose people that looked like her. The PI had described the girl as a five foot, olive skinned thin girl, dark hair with streaks of hot pink hair cut into a Rihanna-esque bobbed style, supersized eyelashes.

Thin? Why is his taste in women crooked these days? She told her PI to inform her of the girl's next appearance, and then ended the call.

She thought of going to Peckham as she had suggested to Athena, but her courage failed her. She was still sceptical about meeting spiritualists, but she was desperate and wished Athena had agreed. She was tired of overlooking her husband's overbearing skirt-chasing marathon; she knew that if he continued at that pace, she may have to walk out of the marriage.

She couldn't risk her children going through the pains and discrimination of divorce; in a society that believes that it's a man's world. Besides, she was still in love with him. And for objectivity; she had to put her daughters first, or at least until she gave him a male child. She believed that she may be able to tolerate his escapades within familiar hours – that way she wouldn't need to know about it, or get wind of it. She wiped her mouth with the back of her hand, and stood up. "It's now or never!"

The next day, soon after the PI had informed her, she decided to go to her husband's office. It was like her heart had fallen to the ground, saying, *God help me.* She got into her car and began a 38 miles journey from High Wycombe to Milton Keynes. She had barely driven ten miles before the car broke down.

She didn't recognise where she was, but knew that it was close to the 1A junction - what annoyed her wasn't the fact that there were no taxi numbers in her phone, but the fact that Olamide had only just fixed the car the two days before. To worsen it, she didn't have a sat-nav nor did she know which bus to take. She wore her winter boots and locked the door. She took a quick look at her watch - it was 11:11. She appraised the car, glad that it was her husband's car. *They may steal it for all I care!*

She flagged down a passing car, which slowed down. the driver gave her the directions she requested. She held her breath, rubbed her face, then tucked her hands in her coat pocket before trudging through the snow.

She headed for Tottenham Hale to take an underground train towards Brixton. She looked down at the black ice and was thankful for dumping her Ugg boots, even though these were tight. Fifty minutes later the second train made a stop at Watford for its passengers to switch trains because it had developed a fault.

She knew a few short routes in Milton Keynes, and decided to take them; the problem was that there was a lot of black ice, which meant she had to back-track a couple of times. By the time she had gotten to her husband's office, she was exhausted, and the girl had gone. She didn't know what to think or say and wondered if that was a good thing.

On her way out of her husband's office, she saw a girl matching the description she was given, in the line formed at one of the cash machines. Temitope joined the line to get a better view of the girl. *What does he even see in her, sef? She is even shorter than I am. She is flat and thin as a broom stick, and...oh I see! It is the breasts!*

The girl's breasts were no less than 38DD and her shifting from one leg to another did nothing to dissipate the eyes ogling her breasts. The girl was fanning herself with a black card. *It must be from one of her lovers. What has she got that others haven't? So much so that Olamide has started keeping late nights!*

The cash machine suddenly looked like it was the only one working as there was a sudden influx, mainly from the male gender to that particular cash machine. This infuriated Temitope even more, but she was too exhausted to care anymore. The girl slipped the card into the machine, crossing and uncrossing her legs continuously as she was waiting for the card to come out.

Temitope cut the line to stand behind the girl then assessed her again, bopping her head at the same time like she was trying to erase the girl. *Useless man! He thinks another girl will get pregnant for him, abi? He had better sort himself out...I could just break this little thwart's head, wring her neck, break every bone in her legs into tiny little splinters. Oh, this stupid girl, this stupid girl! Hurry up, jare, before...*

"No way!" Temitope gasped when she saw her husband's *Visa Signature* card in the girl's hand; it was for an account that her husband had opened in her name to evade tax; she knew every account her husband had opened in her name, even the one with *Eurasian Bank*, courtesy of her private detectives which she'd rather call domestic confidants. *Ah! Imagine o! I myself I don't have the pin.*

A mischievous smile played on her lips as she straightened her back. As soon as the money was out of the machine, her hands were on the girl's hands, tugging at the card and the money. As they struggled, two security guards asked her to let go of the girl, but she ignored them. By the time the security guards got to her, a crowd had ensued. One of the security guards insisted that she let the girl go, and the other collected the items they were squabbling for. Temitope rummaged through her belongings, and quickly produced an ID. They gave the money and the card to her, and apologized.

Olamide will come home early today, at least! As she watched them cart the pugnacious girl away, she started to feel inspired. She hailed a taxi, and went to the mall; her legs started to shake as she stood in front of Ann Summers with hands clasped together, linking her fingers she took quick giant strides into the shop.

All dressed up back at home, she drifted in and out of sleep while waiting for him. She knew it was really late before checking the time on her phone. It was quiet except for the ticking sound from the grandfather clock Olamide bought from the antique shop. The music had stopped playing. She found the ticking of the clock and the hissing sound of the boiler soothing. She called him continuously for about fifteen times, then decided to stop calling; by this time, her hands were shaking and her breathing was heavy. She picked up her phone, and dialled a number.

"I need you to do me a favour."

"Hello!"

"Can you hear me?" Temitope twitched her lips, sounding agitated.

"Yes, you were shouting. I think the network is static."

"Okay. I need you to do me a favour," she repeated, impatiently shaking her legs.

"Okay, Ma'am. Name it."

"I want you to find out where my husband is." She said in a determined tone.

"You already asked us to trail him."

"And...."

"He is in a building, an apartment of some sort in Buckingham. We... I think it's a hostel."

"I want more –"

"Ma'am?"

"Listen." She said, hesitating for a nanosecond. "The girl he is with... I want you to show her what sex really is." She got up, knocking down the champagne bottle down without noticing.

"When?"

"How about now?" she said, almost shouting.

"Em... your husband is there."

"Do with him as you please." She hissed.

"To dust?"

"Hmm?" she retorted, confused.

"To dust. Ma'am you know what I mean."

"He is the father of my children." She replied quickly in horror.

"Point taken."

"Don't bother me with the results."

"As you please and the other stuff."

"As usual." She whispered and ended the call. She never found it conducive to discuss payment over the phone.

Her heart was racing by this time. She went to the bar that demarcated the dining from the sitting room and helped herself to the bottle of vodka closest to her. She opened it before she saw the diagram around the neck of the champagne bottle. An hour later, she received a text, and it read:

> *Couldn't continue as planned - Extenuating Circumstances.*

A second message came as she was deleting the first:

> *A member of my crew is related to the girl in question.*
> *Had to pull her out all the same. Husband left in a cab, heading towards the M47.*
> *Deal accepted as lost.*
> *Apologies.*
> *PS: Need to confirm if other deals are off.*

She twisted her mouth, gulped the shot, and poured herself another before replying.

Fourteen

Athena stirred, but refused to remove the duvet from over her head. She raked the bed, groping at everything except the alarm clock, which she knocked over. It still chimed away. She sighed, peeling off the duvet, lying still for about ten minutes. Then she got up. The winter sun was warm on her face as she opened the window. She felt the urge to pray. Ever since she set her eyes on the book for baby names yesterday, she could think of nothing else.

*I must thank you that I'm still sane. Before I forget, please give me the strength to tolerate my husband and mother-in-law.*She knew her mother-in-law had come in late last night. She overheard Moses telling her to keep her voice down, that his wife was sleeping. Athena promised to thank Bettina for advising her to move back into the room that she shared with her husband; she wondered what she would have had to say or do to salvage her ego, because her mother-in-law would use the opportunity to spite her with reckless abandon. She was glad she hadn't gone for groceries in a while. She hoped her mother-in-law would starve to death.

She dashed to the bathroom to get ready for what she had planned out for the day. Her nose looked swollen in the mirror, but there was nothing to indicate that she was stung, she had gotten used to her face being puffy for some time. *Trust my imagination to spring up dreadful ideas.* She sighed and went downstairs.

She opened the freezer, pulled out the ice cube box, which was shaped like a gun; she had never liked it, but wanted to give her mother-in-law a nudge towards biting her tongue, if it would work. She poured the ice cubes into the jar on the counter, walked into the dining, then leaned on the banister and shouted, "Breakfast is ready!" she shouted before placing the jar of orange juice on the table.

Athena turned around, thinking her husband was trying to surprise her by tiptoeing down the stairs, then heard another set of footsteps this time faster. She gave her mother-in-law an expressionless look, *Oh look, an uninvited guest.* Her gaze shifted from her mother-in-law to her husband who was now behind his mother, silently pleading with his wife to calm down. Athena looked away.

Moses walked briskly into the kitchen, and his mother went to the dining room. Athena went into the dining room with the dessert just in time before her mother-in-law came to the dining table, peering at what was served. Moses pulled out a chair for his mum while Athena pulled out one for herself before he had time to do it for her. He sighed heavily; he could tell she was pissed, and even more so when she started pouring the wine into the glass by herself and playing with it.

Why did this woman have to be here? I have more than enough to deal with already. Athena gave her husband an evil look. *I don't have a say anymore, do I? Anyone can come into my house, our house, when they like? If it was his cousins or even his sister, it would make more sense, but not this woman - who has nothing to do but to chase her son half way across the world to run his marriage. Maybe* she *would have married her son if she had had a chance.*

113

Athena had set the table for two. Afraid of offending his wife, Moses kept quiet; he hadn't had the time to inform his wife of his mother's visit. He leaned over his chair, visibly anxious as he looked down at his wristwatch, then back at the door. Eventually, he started playing with the band of his wristwatch.

Meanwhile, his mother stood aghast, with her jaw dropped open. Finally, she grimaced. *All of these white people without manners, which is the kind of thing my son went to pick up and call 'wife'. Is it not for her own good that she should be married into a decent family like ours? Ah! My mates have grandchildren and I don't even have half a grandchild. Maybe she had done several abortions before.* She shook her head sorrowfully.

Come to think of it, didn't Andrew's daughter do the same thing? Yet she has four children. It's all of these chemicals that they put in their food. Hhm! Moses you should have married a small girl with a good background. I wouldn't be surprised if she has done something so that she will not be tied down with taking care of children.

After all, her mother had been married several times. Anyway, once I show him Wuraola and get them together... hehehe. He is his father's son after all and Wuraola is a very beautiful girl at that unlike this skin and bones that thinks she will be young forever.

She clicked her fingers with a wave. "My son will give me grandchildren anyway possible; you just wait and see."

"Do you have anywhere you have to be?" Athena asked Moses, refusing to look up as she munched the potato hash.

Moses shook his head and sat down; he had to share his food with his mother because he knew that hell would freeze over before he could enter the kitchen to prepare any food, or take food especially on a day like today.

"Hhm!" she said, then buttered her bread. "Someone called you yesterday night."

"Who?" Moses asked.

"Am I supposed to keep track of your calls now?" Athena asked, immediately reprimanding herself for letting her mother-in-law get under her skin. The woman's countenance infuriated Athena even further.

"Look, I'm sorry, okay? Can I have some?" he asked.

Her reply was a warning gaze, which he didn't see because he was staring at her plate.

The dining table was silent except for the sound of crunching food. His mother started mumbling as Athena spread butter on another slice of bread. Athena was tired of taking deep breaths, and counting; she squinted and stared at her husband. He merely shook his head in reply, but didn't talk to his mother.

"My daughter, good morning!"

"Good morning, Ma!" Athena seethed.

"How are you?"

"Fine."

"Why don't you ever call me, 'mummy'?"

That's a new one! "I don't know."

"Then call me, mummy."

"I'll try..." she paused then shook her head. "I'm sorry."

"Give it time –" Moses said.

"Did you say something?" Athena asked, glaring at him coldly.

Moses didn't dare look at his wife's face.

"My daughter, there is something I'll like to discuss with you."

Finally; here it comes! "Okay!" Athena said, getting up.

Her mother-in-law started mumbling again. Athena cleared her side of the table; when she came back to the dining room the woman was still mumbling.

"I'm taking my car to the mechanic."

"When?" Moses asked.

She decided to humour him. "I'll have to get out of these first," she said, tugging at her loungewear.

"Okay. I can give you a lift –" Moses said, getting up after her.

"I'll take a taxi," She responded. Her tone made him sit down. She signalled for him to leave the room so that she could speak with his mother, which he did reluctantly. She crossed her arms, and faced her mother-in-law squarely. "You wanted to talk?"

"Yes. Please sit down."

Athena sat down, leaned back, crossed her legs and with arms still crossed. "Yes?"

"How do I start?" The woman said.

"Straight to the point!" Athena muttered, trying not to look at the grandfather clock behind her mother-in-law.

"What did the doctor say? Have you seen a doctor concerning.... Well, you know I need to hold my grandchildren..."

"We're trying."

"Hhm, if you say so...em...you people are not worried at all at all."

"Worry will not solve the problem. I have gone to see the doctors. Since you care so much why don't you convince your son to do the same?"

"Hahaha, he is potent...." She made a fist "Just like his father and his father before him."

"I see. Well, I guess this discussion is over."

Before Moses' mother could say anything else, Athena was on the stairs.

After about two hours, she came back down the stairs. Moses and his mother were already in the sitting room watching a Nigerian movie. Athena was now wearing a lemon green cotton camisole and a lemon green daisy lace top over dark blue textured chinos shorts with red loafers and a matching red bag.

On her head was an ivory headband with sequined leaves on it, while her blonde hair cascaded down her back. She wore a luscious red lipstick, a colour he was shocked to see on her. Not only had she never worn that colour of lipstick, but she was also wearing a shirt in his favourite colour - a colour she absolutely hated. As if that was not enough, she was wearing shorts.

Shorts? Out of the house? He frowned. *She never wears shorts out of the house; she never lets her hair down. What is she up to? Who is turning her head? She must be seeing someone else. Yes, that must be the reason why she's always out and coming back late. This can't be good, this can't be good.*

He scratched his head, pondering about what she was up to and afraid of what the answer might be. He watched her through the window, walking tall with long, slender endless legs. She was slightly bowlegged and he liked it – it was the exact opposite of his. He was surprised at himself for not being aware of what his wife was like anymore after only five years.

He tried to shake off the feeling that she might be seeing someone else since the person he had hired to keep an eye on her told of no such thing. He couldn't stand still or sit still either. He needed to find out who his wife was seeing and made a mental note to query his friend that was supposed to keep an eye on her. He would possibly have to hire someone better qualified.

He remembered the day they met... *She had dimples; the shape of her eyes reminded him of a tiger's. She had purple hair the day they met. She had claimed she was having a bad hair day. He later discovered she was trying an eccentric look, but couldn't quite pull it off.*

She was posh, plain and simple. There was no way of hiding her better upbringing or her stoic nature. Her lips were shaped like Angelina Jolie's. She hated her nose, and hated plastic surgery, but it was a perfectly sculpted nose; whenever she complained about it, he would kiss it and sometimes pluck it.

He found it intriguing that she was very curvy for a slender woman, and didn't understand why his mother referred to her as 'skin and bones'. Her voice sounded like the echoing of a bell. He had always hated her calling him 'poppet', but now he wished she still did.

He even missed her hand tracing the scar under his shoulder blade, which she called 'scroll', saying it was unique to him. She liked the light on; he didn't like it on when they slept, but now he was used to it. She had always liked the cups faced upwards and glasses faced downwards after washing.

Now they were living like bachelor and spinster.

Fifteen

"Moses! Moses! Moses! How many times did I call you?" His mother asked, trying to sit comfortably in the champagne coloured leather settee.

"Ten times, Mummy!" he said, reluctantly turning away from the window and heading to the kitchen. He absentmindedly poured apple juice into two glasses, letting the sink gulp some.

"What type of chair is this? Couldn't you go yourself instead of sending your wife to get these hard chairs?" She asked, while pouting her mouth and hitting the chair as if that would soften it. Feeling frustrated, she sat down and reduced the volume of the television.

"I got these chairs myself," he said, passing her a glass.

"How many times did I call you?"

Scratching his ear, and fluttering his eyes, "Three times."

"We need to deal with this issue of your childlessness."

"Mummy, please –" he hissed.

"Shut up! 'Please' what? You think you're getting younger?"

"Mummy, we still have time on our –"

"Haa! So it's your plan to wait till I'm in the grave, *abi*?"

"For goodness sake, mummy!" he responded under his breath.

"Don't talk to me like that. In fact, don't talk back at me. I'm still your mother; in case you have forgotten, I carried you and you left me with this..." She raised her blouse to show him the scar across her stomach "... if that is not evidence enough, I nursed you with these breasts." She said, cupping her breasts.

"Yes, you always remind me." He said, wearing a grim face.

"Taah!"

Moses laughed, and she softened a little.

"Come and sit down beside me; let's talk."

"Okay! But mummy, please make it quick."

"Where are you rushing to? Has your wife not gone out?"

"Yes, but I have tennis."

She let out a long hiss, "Instead of saving that strength and using it to service your wife."

Ignoring her comment, he asked, "How about I drop you at the mall on my way out. *I'm not in the mood for this.* How much will you need?" he asked, producing his wallet, and pulling out several leaves of fifty pound notes, "Here, buy something beautiful."

"Don't insult me! I'm doing this for your own good."

"Okay then!"

She snatched the money from his hand before he could replace it in his wallet.

"I'm warning you, oh!" She said and then added calmly, "I have a solution."

Moses laughed hysterically and frowned, "Did you hear that?" he asked, tilting his head for a better reception; hearing nothing else, he shrugged.

"What?"

"Never mind." Moses said, shaking his head.

Athena dropped her bag on the sideboard by the door, and was about to climb the stairs when she heard...

"All you have to do is get another girl pregnant, and I have just the one."

Athena took off her shoes, tiptoeing close to the sitting room.

"Wow, I'm not sleeping with another woman."

"Oh, shut up! I know you're seeing another woman on the side, but these London girls are rip-offs, and some already have husbands back home. I tell you, they'll even sell the clothes on your back."

"Where do you get these ideas from?" Moses asked, now scratching the nape of his neck.

"Never mind how; what you need to know now is that I have a solution."

Moses got up, laughing. "I need to go now. I'll see you later!" He bent down to kiss his mother, but she caught his arm.

"I brought a girl with me; she is sleeping upstairs."

His jaws dropped as he stared at his mother in shock.

"Don't look at me like that! She came in very early this morning because there was no ticket for her to come with me."

"What? From where? This is not Nigeria o! How the hell did she get in?"

"I know, and don't use such words. I didn't want to create a scene, knowing you people can be very funny. So I brought her so that you can, you know..." She pulled him closer, and lowered her voice "...I want you to impregnate her."

"What the hell?" Moses said, almost shouting. He tried to slip away, but his mother tightened her grip.

"Why are you behaving like a small child *sef*? It's not like your wife was the first girl you slept with. Wait till you see her..." She said, laughing lightly. "I know what you like, you know! This one is fresh and practically untouched."

"Oh my God!" he said in mock horror.

She let go of his hand, knowing that he was considering it; after all, he didn't have just his father's looks. "Don't worry, I'll take care of your wife while you go to visit the girl..." she nudged him, smiling mischievously, "...you know what I mean nawh!"

"I can't even believe you're suggesting that I... You're the President of the women's organization in church for goodness sake."

"Yes, oh! Mh-huh! To women who have already held their great-grandchildren."

"I'm not going to hear the end of this, am I?" he muttered.

"No oh, of course not! I won't stop until you listen to the voice of a wise woman," then she started striking her chest. "Ahh! If your father were alive, you would have had a second, even a third wife by now." She raised her right hand to her back, rocking herself left to right, and simultaneously clicking her middle finger and thumb.

"This is the end of this discussion." Moses said, sternly.

"Anyway, where is the money I asked for?" she asked, carelessly.

"But you just took... it's in your account."

"These few pounds?" she asked, waving the notes at him. "When did you send it?"

"Yesterday afternoon."

"Then I didn't get it because I checked my account this morning."

"Mummy, it's there; I asked my –"

"Your wife?"

"My assistant, mummy -"

"Your wife... the white witch that wants to enjoy your money, and not give you children..." Then she started wailing.

Moses briskly walked away.

"The one that won't give me grandsons, even if it is just... one." As soon as she heard the door click shut, she punched numbers into the telephone, which was set on the rosewood side table beside her. She was still talking on the phone, when a young girl of no more than eighteen years of age wearing a worn-out, oversized shirt, walked into the sitting room, stretching and yawning.

"Get ready; I want you to take me to a very good salon...two people. He doesn't have a choice. Be ready to take us shopping too.

"Mama, good morning." The girl said as soon as Moses' mother replaced the phone.

"Good morning, my dear. Did you sleep well?"

"Yes ma; I just have a small headache sha."

"I'll get my son to give you Panadol ..." Then she hissed. "Oh, he went out moments ago. Go, get ready, we have somewhere to go."

Moses' mother knew she needed to nudge her son a bit more to speed up the process; in other words, she needed the strategic appetite of a woman's prowess to make it happen. She watched the girl leave while she tapped her fingers on the glass of juice .

A few minutes later, the girl came back in a black and purple tie and dye kaftan over black footless tights.

Athena unconsciously used her tongue to clean her teeth, annoyed that the girl's teeth were brilliantly white and well set. She almost forgot that she was scrambling on the floor. *I'm going to win my husband back to myself alone. I'm done with self-pity.* She got up, dried her eyes, straightened her back and marched into the sitting room.

"Oh! My daughter, welcome! You are already back from the mechanic?" Moses' mother said to Athena through gritted teeth.

"No, I forgot something."

"Good morning, Ma!" the new girl said.

"Good morning ..."

"Wura." The new girl said and curtsied.

"Good morning Wura! How are you?"

"Fine, Ma!"

"Please call me Athena." She stretched out her hand, and smiled broadly when Wura put her hand in hers.

Wura looked at Athena strangely. *Okay! She is a fine white woman; who is she? I wonder why Mama is calling her 'my daughter'?*

"Welcome to my home. I'm going out in a bit, but my husband's mother will take care of you. Feel free to call me if you need me. Hope you will be staying!" Athena smiled brilliantly.

Wura stared at Athena as she left then turned to face her soon-to-be mother-in-law. "You didn't tell me he was married. Why didn't you tell me?" Wura asked in a loud whisper.

"What's that to you?"

"I will not be a second wife to any man," Wuraola stuttered.

"My dear, do you think that most men who come here remain single waiting for a Nigerian wife? However, I guarantee, that if you should get pregnant for my son, you'll be the only wife. I promise I'll take care of you."

"I'm not liking this one bit – "

"You don't have to like, just do. Don't forget I've paid handsomely for this arrangement."

"I'll do as you say," she said reluctantly. *It's not like I have another choice!*

"Do me proud."

Athena heard everything, and started crying again. *Snap out of it! Crying never solved anything!*

Sixteen

She stopped swirling the gin and tonic she had in her hand. The smile that crossed her lips gradually turned to a grin. She frowned, clasping the glass in two hands, got up quickly, rushed into the toilet, and puked. *Even gin? I must have a stomach bug, but first things first.* She shuddered and delved into her bag to get a wet wipe, then glanced at her reflection. She touched the skin around her eyes; all of the weeping had left her with swollen eyes and dark circles that makeup could no longer conceal. She had called in a friend who was now at the bar ordering a glass of J20.

He is already greying. "Water?" she asked, jokingly.

"Still working." He said casually, then pulled out a stool beside hers. He looked over his shoulder; following her gaze, before they went to sit down in a dimly lit corner that someone had just vacated.

"It's been a while," she said, looking down, but he didn't notice.

"I know. I was surprised to see your number."

"I'm surprised that you still have my number."

"Do you want something?" he asked her.

"Not sure, was considering a burger."

"Considering?"

"Yeah, sort of...." *Can't afford to make another visit to the loo.*

"Burger it is. Chicken or beef?"

"Chicken. Thanks!"

Ten minutes later he was back.

"Wow that was fast!"

"I jumped the queue." He said, laughing.

"Good to see you haven't changed." She replied, smiling as past memories were rekindled. He ate while she pushed her plate aside.

"I will make this quick. Here is what I need, and I don't want the person to be aware of it being administered." She slipped him a piece of paper which he quickly read, then handed back to her.

"What is this?" he asked, knowing what it was.

"You owe me, and I've come to collect."

"What the hell are you talking about?"

"Do we want to discuss this one?"

He got up.

"How about your aliases, 'swanky', 'slimy entosë', do you need me to go on?"

"How?"

"Not important." *I'm surprised you don't even know your daughter? Doctor Nathaniel Mendez, it's your fault my mum went berserk, marrying any man she could get hold off...*

"For how long?" Doctor Nathaniel Mendez asked.

"As long as possible."

"Because one of them requires a minor surgery. It's complicated."

Athena rubbed her cheek. "I want it uncomplicated."

"The injection lasts for three months but it can make you...the person gain weight rapidly -."

"Get me those ones and all I'll need to make it a smooth process." She slid off of the stool.

"But –" The doctor followed her movement.

"But what?" She turned abruptly, hitting him slightly.

"What name?"

"Think of something that wouldn't get you in trouble. I'll tell you where we will meet after you've..." She got up stiffly.

She sauntered out through the back door, entering the taxi the doctor had come with while he entered hers in front of the pub. She felt sure she was being followed, and told the driver to circle the street twice before taking her to her destination. He parked on a street lay-by and then she paid him. She looked around until her eyes caught the narrow path which led to the address she was looking for. At the end of the narrow road, she turned left, passed through a small gate, then walked through a path beside a private residence.

She repulsed his advances back when she was in university. *Doctor Nathaniel Mendez, she knew who he was as soon as she set her eyes on him. She was working in one of the university's libraries at the time. He was a lecturer that was brought in to take care of Dr Parkins' course: Women in Psychology. She observed him through his stay. Women came and went as they pleased: he was handsome. It was even rumoured that he slept with them in the office.*

Three weeks later his pattern changed. He started coming to the library often. It started with returning a book, and coming back an hour later for the same book, making sure he had reserved it well in advance. Then he started sending flowers.

On one occasion, Valentine's Day, he sent her two dozen flowers, embarrassing all of the women that worked there, because each bouquet was one of their favourites. They always went to receive, and later discovered that the package was in Athena's name. They all knew that she was allergic to flowers, so at the end of the day's work, each took one for herself, even Cosmos; the school's bus driver on duty had one to take to his wife.

Dr Mendez saw them leave at the end on the day, each carrying his flowers.

Meanwhile, Athena was in the Maldives with a few friends who had no boyfriend, and who didn't want to be pressured into 'hanging out'.

A month later, as she was replacing the books she had taken off of the desk someone tickled her. She let go of the heavy books, and screamed simultaneously. It was during the exam weeks and the library was filled with students. That was his last day.

She never told her mother that she had met her father or how she knew him. She was lost in thought; she wasn't looking until she was startled back into reality by a dog barking a few feet away from her in the middle of the path.

She felt her heart drop from her chest when she heard it rattle its chain. It fought vigorously with the chain as it barked; all she could see was its teeth as saliva spurted out of the muscular dog. Its eyes seemed to be saying 'come let me devour you'. Someone spoke from behind her, she jumped and fell, twisting her ankle in the process, it was only then that she realised that she had wandered into someone's residence. She felt barricaded between the dog and its owner who was twice her size and stank of alcohol.

The urge to explain enveloped her, but it sounded like she was chanting. The owner of the dog kept scratching his two-tone beard. He only heard the address she was heading to everything else was gibberish.

When she finally opened her eyes, he was pointing to the back of the house adjacent to his. She nodded her thanks, almost running. She couldn't bring herself to admit her fear; she tried to steady her breath as she walked briskly through the cobbled street to the girl's house.

When she arrived at the house of the girl rumoured to have been her husband's distraction, she pressed the doorbell twice to be sure no one was home. She stood on the semi-porch facing the road, pondering her next move, wondering if it was wise to ask the neighbour about the girl in question. She also queried herself on what she would do if she saw the girl, then someone tapped her on the shoulder.

She looked down to see an old woman holding a gas cylinder standing beside her and frowned.

"Are you all right, dear?" the old woman asked squinting. Her smile revealed a toothless gum which would have been cute on a little child.

"I am." Athena answered, reluctant to have a conversation with the woman.

"Why don't you join me for a cup of tea?" The old woman asked, not noticing Athena's reluctance.

"I have —"

"I could use the company," the woman interrupted before walking back to her house, struggling with her cylinder.

Out of courtesy, Athena helped her carry it, but with contempt. By the end of two hours all she found out was that the girl always had regular visitors, one who came between 12pm to 2pm and the other between 5.30pm to 8pm. It was better than nothing even though the information did nothing to give her relief. Her husband was always back by six in the evening. She had a nagging feeling that the woman wasn't sure of what she was saying, so she decided to wait until twelve noon.

By eleven-thirty, a lanky boy with reddish-brown tousled hair left the house, and went to the house under the old woman's. Twenty minutes later a black Mercedes Benz parked in front of the building, but because of how small and closely situated the houses were. She couldn't tell which house the guest was heading to. She couldn't shake off the feeling, that the lanky boy was familiar. There was something about him, something she couldn't quite grasp. She thought of going out there to meet the driver; her legs were shaking so much she stayed put.

Athena would have confronted the driver if she had had the courage, mainly because her husband also had that kind of car. The position of the car didn't let her see its number plate. The tension was becoming so unbearable that she decided to go to ask the driver when the car door opened. The driver turned slightly to make way for the passenger to come out.

She rubbed her eyes: *I'm not dreaming am I? Olamide is her 12pm appointment. Who is this fucking girl? For one, I didn't know he had a new car. Why is he always complaining about not having money to pay the mortgage? The car must be the reason my husband refused to lend him the money last night. Oh my! What will Temi think of this? I'm certainly not the one to tell. My goodness, she'll tear this girl limb from limb. Why doesn't she come out so I can take a look at her?*

At two o'clock she went to the window; pulling the thin and muslin-like curtain up slightly, she saw the car drive by. There was a honk and Olamide came out of the house, holding his phone to his ear. The car sped away as soon as he was inside it. The old woman was right.

After all, who wouldn't be with the cry-out remedy on the opposite side of the wall beside them; it was a cure for sleepiness, even the walls had a potent analysis of that.

What did Moses see in this girl? What has she got that I haven't got? I mean, it's not like I was a robot in bed? Imagine all of the tricks I had to learn, to please him and how does he repay me? By raping me, that's how? Oh! What have I not done for him? Where would he have been, without me? After he wasted his money, who was there to bail him out? If he wants a doormat, didn't he know that I wasn't one? Is this what marriage does to people? Take away your personality, even your peace of mind?

She waited until 2:15pm by which time she had cleaned, replaced most of the old woman's things, and poured her heart out profusely. This was probably the reason the poor woman fell asleep on the couch. Annette felt sorry for the woman, and made her comfortable before leaving.

On her way out of the old woman's house, the boy with the tousled hair walked briskly back to the house. He had disappeared into the house before she got to him. A woman jogging past had a very cute hairy dog. Athena couldn't help smiling at it. In response the dog came frolicking around her, seemingly in the mood to flirt with someone else. Athena knelt down to play with the dog before she realised she hadn't asked politely. She apologized, but the woman waved it aside, jogging on the spot while her dog slobbered all over Athena's face. *If only I could own a dog, at least it'll be trustworthy!* She sighed, thanked the woman just before sliding into the taxi.

Every day, one argument to another just to make sure that I obey his every wish, I think he started cheating on me because I've been too submissive, but now he's not going to get easy. Moses you've changed and so have I! Welcome to a brand new me!

♥♥♥

She looked up at the building. It was modern with full front glass walls. It looked like an office rather than a dentistry. The receptionist was rifling through a filing cabinet impatiently. Athena tapped the bell, then smiled down at the receptionist who was now admiring her perfume.

"Hello! How may I help?"

"I have a four o'clock appointment."

"Which Doctor?"

"Dr. Humphreys, please."

The receptionist nodded and picked up the phone. She covered the mouth piece, "The doctor will be a little late. Please wait and look at that sign for when your name comes up." When Athena was about to leave she asked, "Sorry, what perfume is that?"

"Jadore!" she answered, before thinking. *What is wrong with the smell? This is the only perfume that hasn't sent me to the toilet.* She placed her hand on her chest, wondering why she suddenly felt jittery.

"Wow, it's so beautiful!" The receptionist slowly sniffed the air around her desk.

Athena backed away amused, picking up the pace while trying to walk quietly. She walked into the dentist's office, and three hours later she had finished with the fillings and air-flow brushing. By the time the dentist had finished the filings and the airflow brushing it was 6.30pm. The dentist didn't do teeth bleaching or zoom-whitening, but she made an arrangement for it; she didn't care that it was a thirty minutes' drive.

Gratefully, it was Thursday; the mall at Milton Keynes would be open until 8pm. She checked her wallet, then decided to go for some requisition in the mall, making a mental note to stop at *House of Frazer* after getting some scones from *M&S*.

Athena felt she had been through enough for one day, fortunately, her appointment for zoom whitening was fixed for the following day. She was more concerned with the excuse she was going to pass off for missing Moses' tennis tournament. She had placed the order for thongs from *Ann Summers* because her husband loved them. She was going to seduce him until he crawled on his knees, begging, and if he tried to her rape her, she had a plan. She prepared a specially toxic pepper spray for him.

She heard her mother-in-law's voice as soon as soon as she entered the house; the door separating the hallway from the sitting room was wide open.

She quickly shoved her *Ann Summers* bag into the *Hawes and Curtis* bag when it didn't fit into her *House of Frazer* one. She didn't realise how tired she was until she got to her room. Her feet had grown three times their size; she laughed at how shiny and smooth they looked, and blamed it on water retention. Later she put everything she bought in her closet, soaking her feet in cold water after taking her bath. She kept a pair of socks on the chest of drawers by the bed, in case she caught a chill.

♥♥♥

Athena started wearing only lingerie around the house, and flimsy little silk dressing gown when she went out of the room.

One Saturday morning, she went to the gym in the loft for about an hour. She was sweating, with nothing underneath, her white t-shirt. She ran into the bathroom, turned on the shower, then came out to towel her hair dry.

She knew Moses was in the bathroom, watching her from the mirror in front of him. He made a sound between clearing his throat, and sighing so she wouldn't think he was watching her.

She kept seducing him for weeks, but when his efforts to return the favour were not remunerated: the available became the desirable.

Seventeen

"Here!" Temitope handed Athena a glass of water.

"Thanks!" Athena took the glass of water which she hurriedly gulped down.

"My dear, take it easy, there's more water, eh? You know..." Temitope pushed a throw pillow away from her sinking gently into the chair. "We need to go shopping."

"What did you do?" Nadine looked at her with mock suspicion.

"What do you mean? And why are you looking at me like that?" Temitope snapped.

Nadine wasn't perturbed by her outburst. "You are struggling to sit down."

"Oh! My sister, I don't know what I ate o, but it must have had a lot of pepper because since yesterday night hmm..."

All of the women started laughing.

"Hello ladies!" Nadine's husband walked in cheerily.

"Fine, thank you! We are happy to see you! God bless you!" they all chorused.

Thrown aback, he frowned, but it was directed at Athena.

"We are teaching her something we learnt in school." Nadine said, and got up to greet her husband, then disappeared by the winding stairs.

"Before Nadine rudely interrupted me –"

"Haba Temi! I never even comot before you begin dey gossip me, na wa oh!" Nadine's arms were akimbo, her stomach still looking big.

"Anyway... as I was saying before she..." Temitope turned to point at Nadine. "Rudely interrupted me a second time, you have been drinking a lot of water –"

"You've even added weight, and you're no longer going to the gym." Nadine finished, smiling triumphantly at Temitope.

"You see how she is always trying to steal my show? No respect whatsoever." Temitope demonstrated.

"Girls, take it easy before the baby wakes up." Nadine's husband said in a loud whisper, revealing only his head and legs from the stairs.

"Yes, Daddy!" Temitope and Athena spoke in unison and started laughing. He shook his head, smiling and climbed back up.

"How did you meet?" Temitope asked Nadine.

"Wow! It's an interesting story, but not one for today, you know." Nadine said, pointing upstairs.

"I get!" Temitope whispered to Athena pointing upwards. "The man of the house."

"What? Oh!" Athena nodded, not understanding what she meant.

"What do you fancy in Moses?"

"Why me?" Athena paused "Okay, he makes me laugh and I love a good *nata*!" she smiled to herself, her eyes lighting up simultaneously.

The other two looked coyly at each other.

"But?" The other two women, sat upright, and listened intensely.

"Oh, nothing! It's just embarrassing. I mean, Nadine taught me to cook some Nigerian delicacy. So I did, but forgot the food on the stove. Funny enough, it was not smelling, at least not until I opened the pot."

They all laughed loudly, then softly when they remembered the baby was sleeping.

"What was his expression?" Temitope asked, still laughing.

"Stop interrupting." Nadine slapped Temitope lightly.

"I don't know... couldn't look at his face! So, to make up for it I got Nadine to ask him his favourite meal. I think he suspected because he never gave it up until after the wedding. I haven't summoned up enough courage since then."

"Are you serious? After making me lose over three weeks of normal sleep?" Nadine jumped out of her seat.

"Yeah, we all know your normal sleeping hours." Athena said smiling.

"After five years?" Temitope asked.

"I can't believe it!" Nadine said in a hushed voice.

Athena nodded and smiled apologetically at Nadine, who waved it aside.

Nadine plopped on the chair. "You have to cook us something. Do you have foodstuff?"

"From today, you will no longer be skittish, in Jesus' name. Amen!"

Athena laughed.

"Say Amen!" Nadine said, sternly.

"Amen. But seriously though...."

"Ah! Ah! Ah..." Nadine waved a finger at her. "You are cooking and we are eating."

"So what is she cooking?" Temitope asked.

"I'm still here, hello!"

"Okay! What are you cooking?"

"I don't know!" Athena said, slowly, looking distracted.

Nadine sniggered while Temitope shook her head.

"What do I cook?"

"That is an excellent question. What should she cook?" Temitope asked Nadine again.

"Tell us which one, Egusi, Ogbono, Okazi, you know... think of one."

"Let's make a list," Temitope said.

"Yes, what's the time....hmn! I better go and shake off that man upstairs. Remember, we're not doing big shopping today, just enough to cook one dish for now. Okay?"

"Well that's good then, hurry up! We don't have all day!" Athena got up.

"Look who's talking...." Temitope said.

Athena made a dash for the toilet.

"*Abegi*, close your mouth, you too dey chance pesin." Nadine came back and sat beside Temitope just as Athena returned, wiping her mouth.

Temitope and Nadine stared at Athena then at each other, then gave Athena a hug before they started jumping and giggling.

"I thought you wanted to meet your Oga at the top?" Temitope nudged Nadine.

"That's true o! BRB!"

"What were you jumping and giggling about?"

"You don't know and you joined in?"

"Well..."

"You're cooking for us aren't you? Because we are not going to rejoice and you kill it."

"Wow, sure, I guess."

♥♥♥

The following day Athena received a call around 6 o'clock in the morning, and drove out to meet the doctor. He handed her the package through his window to hers. Neither of them got out of their car. She nodded her thanks, and they drove off in opposite directions.

After driving for about ten minutes, she parked her car and reclined the driver's seat. She stared blankly at the package, afraid of opening it. Her heart raced when she thought of what she'd have to do. Suddenly feeling tired and sleepy, she rubbed her eyes and sat up.

She was still driving at 40mph on a 30mph road until she was forced to swerve off of the road when another car sped towards her. Luckily, there was no speed camera in the area. She killed the engine, still holding the steering wheel like her life depended on it, and at the same time she tried to catch her breath. She was glad she had done some work on the car, and wound down the window.

The smell of burnt tires made her want to retch. She quickly scrambled out of the car, and did just that. She never believed in signs, but felt this was a warning. Sighing, she opted to abort her plans for Wura.

The sun was rising just as she got home.

She looked around the garden, making a mental note to call a landscape gardener. With parcel in hand, she walked to the bin. She looked inside, and changed her mind because it was empty. She decided to wait it out until Tuesday when the bins would be collected.

She heard laughter coming out of the sitting room; they were speaking Yoruba language. She was about to push the door open when she heard Wura let out a throaty laugh. Athena pushed the door open slightly, to see her husband leaning in the direction of Wura like he was about to whisper something to her. Athena's courage was restored.

Later the following day, she brought the package out of her knickers' drawer. It was already twelve noon: Moses and his mother had been out for about an hour, and wouldn't be back for at least four hours if they didn't stay for the wedding reception. Athena didn't go because she didn't want to be around her mother-in-law.

Wura didn't go with them because she had developed a stomach bug – what actually happened was that Athena wanted to take some laxatives but it slipped into Wura's juice which was directly under the cabinet she kept medicine in; no one saw it so she decided to remedy it by replacing the juice but by the time she got back, but Wura had greedily gulped it down.

The die was cast, and she didn't want to waste the opportunity that had readily presented itself. She walked quietly down the stairs. Needing to be on the safe side, she locked the door from the inside, and stiffened when Wura stirred in her sleep. After a few seconds she tiptoed towards the bed. Her heartbeat was deafening, but she had gone too far to turn back now. She stepped on something, and in reaction to the sudden pain, she jumped, instantly landing on Wura's legs.

Wura involuntarily kicked her legs. She quickly covered Wura's face with a handkerchief soaked through and through with chloroform, waited for a few minutes before removing her hand from over Wura's mouth. Athena sighed deeply several times to steady her breath.

Not wanting to waste any more time, she opened a brown paper bag, brought out the syringe already filled with *Depo Provera*, inserted the needle on the prepared syringe, injected Wura on her left arm with precision via her experience in giving Nadine's mum insulin shots.

She picked up the brown wrapper, left the room, then quickly went to the kitchen, and dropped everything. She took the bin out, smiling mischievously because the bin would be taken away the following day. She felt relieved, but was now shaking uncontrollably as the adrenalin started to subside.

My husband is mine and mine alone! My marriage may not be the best but by God I'm not pulling out; not now, not yet! She considered taking a long bath and felt it would be worthwhile. She must have dozed off for a long time because she woke up to find herself lying snugly in her husband's arms.

She was still angry, and tried to wiggle out, but his arm was firmly around her – her anger wasn't directed at him, but to herself for wanting him, craving him. She needed to remain where she was at that moment: in his arms. She exhaled as he burrowed his head in her hair, and sighed. *We are going to be all right!* Smiling smugly, she drifted off to sleep.

♥♥♥

"What did you even see in her?" his mother asked as they waited their turn for the buffet. "I mean your wife."

"She was the most beautiful girl I had ever set my eyes on." Moses smiled dreamily.

"Oh jare! Is that not the same thing you said about Johnson's daughter? Then you went for the Ambassador's daughter, then you went for... what is the name of that girl that had very skinny legs, and a very large sweaty and flaring nose, then that girl I never got to see that you met in the plane. Besides, your wife had purple hair then, remember?"

"Seriously this was different, and still is. So she had a bad hair day, big deal!" *Her eyes, oh her eyes!* His mother tapped him.

"Did she tell you that?"

"Why are we discussing my wife?"

"Look..." She held him back, whispering, "I'm not asking you to divorce her! I'm only saying you can sow some wild oats just to... you know... test the waters with another woman who could create the magic. I have made it easier by providing one from a family with a very good background. I tell you no one...." She paused, then stepped aside for a lady in headgear twice the size of her head to get through. "No one in her father's house or her mother's house has ever had issues with getting pregnant, and they are very strong women too. Just enter her once, and she will do the magic. I promise you."

"I hate complications."

"And there'll be none." She responded immediately.

Moses sniggered.

"Ehen Moses, please remember we have another wedding to attend next month o. So, don't forget to remind me. Ehen! Like as I was saying, all you have to do is keep trying till Wuraola gets pregnant; as soon as she gets pregnant, I'll take her back to Nigeria with me. Your wife will not even know about it, and you can come from time to time to see your child. You're a Yoruba man. You shouldn't be complaining about taking a second wife. Besides, a lot of men will be dying to be in your shoes right now, with an offer such as this."

"I thought you loved me because I was different from other men."

"I do, son, it's your father's stubbornness in you that I hate."

Eighteen

She could tell that Bettina was shouting at someone, and it sounded like a heated argument, but she couldn't just walk away because she had already pressed the bell. She was still contemplating leaving when Bettina's son opened the door, and welcomed her in. The sound of the door banging made her jump slightly.

"Are you all right?" Bettina frowned.

Athena nodded.

"You were a bit jumpy. So what is going on?"

"Apart from the fact that my mother-in-law is trying hard to get her to seduce my husband, everything is peachy."

"Wait o! And you are here?" Bettina sounded alarmed.

"I need to clear my head."

"My dear, you have cleared your head on your way here, on your way back, work on a solution. Understand?"

"Are you driving me away?"

"Yes, go home, think and write everything you saw in your husband. Check yourself, see your flaws and see what you did wrong before pointing fingers. Remember it takes two for the marriage to work. Now that he is making a change, assist him."

"Seriously?"

"Yes seriously."

"This is not fair!" Athena stomped her feet.

"Life is not fair. Now go home and do as I say."

"You're taking his side?"

"In marriage there are no sides my dear. Oya go home."

Annoyed, she went back to her car, and drove aimlessly for three hours. Then she started heading back home, driving slowly this time and ignoring the horns blaring behind her.

♥♥♥

As soon as she walked in, the light came on.

"Thank you." Athena mumbled, walking away from the switch near the door.

She looked up to see a familiar and unauthorised person in her room. *What the hell? Moses, where is that fucking son of a bitch?* She got a hint of her husband's perfume and knew he must have been in the room.

"Moses! How did you find where the switch was?" Athena asked.

Wura winced when the bedroom door closed.

"What switch?" she stammered, acting aloof.

"That one! You see, it took me two whole weeks to find that socket."

"So?"

"Ahh! I'll tell you! You see, it's in an obscure position and the only way you could have known where it is, is if you were here when my husband was around to see him put it on, or he showed you how to put it on. Which one is it?" Athena's face by now was as red as strawberry as she tugged her scarf off her neck, and threw it on the bed.

Wura's eyes moved from Athena to the door.

Athena in a deft movement was at the door. After locking the door, she dropped the key inside her bra, thankful for the idea she got from a Nigerian movie which she was practically forced to watch. Then she advanced towards Wura who backed away quickly, shouting out, but unknown to her the walls in their house were dense; the bedroom was the most dense.

"Did I invite you into this room?" Athena unhooked her red glossy tote and tossed it aside.

143

Wura kept mute, shaking her head and continuing to back away.

"I don't hear an answer!" Athena kicked off her shoes, then went straight to Wura with arms held in a boxing stance.

Wura crouched into a defensive mode. "He invited me, I swear." She was afraid of fighting back not just because her friends had told her that fighting a white person could cause her to be sent to prison, but also because she didn't stand a chance since she couldn't fight.

"Really?"

"Stay away from me." Wura shouted, pointing a warning finger at her.

"Make me." And her hand hit Wura straight on the left eye. She staggered, but didn't fall. Athena jumped on her, pulling them to the floor. Athena punched her on the back nonstop, wanting her to turn so that she could get the face and kept squealing, "I don't share."

She didn't notice that Wura had been crawling under her until she hit her head on the table at the other end of the room. Wura quickly freed herself, and tried to force the oak wood door open. Athena ignored the throbbing pain, and rushed at Wura, yanking her away from the door by pulling on her braids.

"Aw! Aw! Kai! Kai! Kai!" Wura wailed, and tried to free her hair from Athena's firm grip. Sadly, she did not succeed. She wiggled into Athena, giving her a head butt, and they both fell on the bed.

Athena became furious as the thought of Wura in bed with her husband flashed in her mind. "You're dead!" Athena rolled on top of Wura. She started bitch-slapping her while Wura tried to grab her opponent by the hair, which was neatly wrapped in a bun; not succeeding, she tried to reach the face which was equally unsuccessful because Athena's body was slightly turned away from her. Wura's screams and cries for help brought back memories of her inability to scream when her husband assaulted her; this infuriated Athena who turned wild and started scratching Wura's face and pulling Wura's braids again.

When Wura couldn't take it anymore, she launched forward and grabbed the loops of the tie of Athena's shirt and held onto it tightly, tugging it, and then pushed Athena off of her, and the key fell out. In a nanosecond, the key entered the slot, Wura turned it, and ran out of the room.

Athena sat on the bed, feeling winded and trying to catch her breath. She considered going after Wura, and decided to let her go. Then she remembered that her mother-in-law went for a wedding, and if she knew her well she would be the last to leave the venue.

She jumped off of her bed, and ran down the stairs. When she got to the landing, she remembered the keys to the other rooms in the house, and ran back up. Then she returned to lock all of the exit doors. Relieved, she walked purposefully towards the room she knew Wura would be in, and unlocked it. She knew Wura wasn't stupid, and could be waiting behind the door so she peered through the crack as she cautiously pushed the door open slowly.

She stepped aside as Wura ran towards her with a large green encyclopaedia. Before Wura could stop, she went over the railing head first with the encyclopaedia in hand. Athena, wide-eyed, stood beside the banister and looked down to see Wura rubbing her elbows and crying and with her shoulders slumped; she had fallen into a sofa that was moved out of position.

This girl could well be my sister. She is only doing this because... well she just might be desperate. Athena walked down the stairs quietly, not to startle her, then slid to the ground, taking Wura in her arms. They both wept; relieved for different reasons.

"I'm sorry!" they chorused quietly, sapped, leaning on the wall and staring into space.

"Friends? Please?" Wura touched Athena's arms gently.

Athena hesitated, "Friends." *What have I got to lose? I can keep track of her activities as a friend.* She gave Wura's hands a firm squeeze.

Wura gave her a grateful smile.

"Why did you come?"

"If you must know: I had no other choice that's why I took the offer. She came just in the nick of time. You see six years ago I was dating this guy... anyway his mother didn't like me, and so she paid me off. I took the money because the guy in question was useless. I left most of it in the bank until I gained admission into university. My parents later found out, and it caused serious problems for me so I decided to make it up to them. I promised to go back to school but since the money is finished. Your mother-in-law came along and it was... you know the rest. I didn't know he was married until you introduced yourself."

"How many years have you got?"

"I have just one year to finish studying law."

"Law seems to be a Nigerian thing, no offence though."

"None taken. I don't know why. They probably study it because they still believe it's the most prestigious profession after medicine."

"What do you think?"

"I'll let you know in ten years' time."

They were silent for a while.

"You should have asked me?" Athena asked.

"How? I didn't know you before I came here!"

"Trust my mother-in-law." Athena muttered.

"Did you say something?"

Athena shook her head, "Just that it's true... our not knowing each other and the circumstances too. Let's change that story. Shall we call a truce?" Athena asked.

They looked at each other and chorused, laughing, "Yes, we shall!"

"But for this to work, my mother-in-law and husband cannot know."

Wura nodded.

"Truth is, your husband is handsome."

Athena raised her brow scrutinising Wura then said ruefully, "Tell me about it."

Wura frowned.

For the first time in a while Athena's smile was about her husband.

Nineteen

There was unaccustomed peace in the sitting room as Athena prepped for her knitting project, her mother-in-law watched *Looney Toons* on *Channel 5* while Wura was reading an Agatha Christie novel. Athena winked at Wura who giggled; pretending it was something from what she was reading when her mother-in-law looked at her. Athena laughed lightly at first, and then louder, drawing her mother-in-law's attention to her. She was oblivious to the woman eyeing her scornfully.

In frustration, the mother-in-law pounded the buttons of the remote control. *My girl Wura will give my son a son very soon!* Athena's mother smiled dreamily; I'll then carry my grandchild. Oh no stopping there because I will carry more grandchildren.

They all turned to the loud bang. Athena's mother-in-law opened the curtain, and quickly went to the door, but Moses had already turned his key in the lock. As soon as Moses closed the door, he started to sneeze. Athena affixed her ear piece, and with a drink in hand went upstairs, but the music was mute. She knew her husband would soon be in need of her assistance.

Fifteen minutes later, there was banging on her door. She would have told them that he was allergic to dogs when her mother-in-law's friend brought it in but she wanted to have the last laugh. They had tried to call the hospital, but Athena had had to end the contract with the subscriber the week before, after her mother-in-law used up a year's worth of credit in two days. When she came out, her husband's face was twice its size.

She couldn't help laughing because he reminded her of *Tim Carrey* in *Megamind*. Athena went to the medicine cabinet in their bathroom while his mother and Wura set him on the bed. She came back, and drove them out of her room which they obliged before locking the door behind them. He stretched his arms out to her and she didn't hesitate, because she had added a sleeping pill to the medication she handed him.

♥♥♥

Athena fiddled with the carnations, pulling each petal, and crushing it before going for another. "I can't take this any longer," she said out loud, throwing the napkin down carelessly. The slight force shook the water in the vase on a picture beside it. It was their wedding picture. She sat there staring at it, wishing it would evoke an emotion, *any emotion*. She brought it closer, peered at it, then set it down. Just then the doorbell rang. She ignored it, but went to the door when it rang the second time.

She had just finished cleaning when Moses walked into the room with two dozen blue roses and one dozen black roses. His voice boomed over her as he asked her if she wanted to eat out.

Athena nodded. She tried to steady herself; he always had a way of taking her breath away both negatively *and* positively. As soon as she felt sure she was calm enough to speak without faltering, she sighed, turned around and froze. He was on the phone making a reservation.

He had bought roses, and worst of all black ones. He only discovered his mistake when he saw her shocked face, and followed her gaze to the flowers. He stood at the door like a robot. He knew she knew that his mother wasn't the type you get flowers for, unless it was made of Swarovski crystals; Wura who, well... she simply did know that giving flowers is a sign of affection. He wouldn't dare lie about it being Olamide's mistake because his wife didn't do flowers, worst of all black roses.

She almost couldn't suppress a giggle as she watched his reaction.

Moses avoided his wife's gaze. He was afraid of moving, wishing at that moment that he could be transported back to the moment before he walked into the bedroom, giving him enough time to ditch the flowers.

Her giggle quickly faded, and she started biting her lips the way she always did to prevent words she could not take back from slipping out.

♥♥♥

Olamide had gone to the toilet several times. Temitope knew he was up to something. She wasn't keen on finding out, though.

Within an hour, he had played *Candy Crush Saga*, drank two glasses of water and a glass of raspberry juice, each time lingering in the kitchen, and finally a shot of whisky. Ten minutes later, he resorted to flipping the newspaper nosily to gain his wife's attention. Instead she switched on the sound system.

He started to totter on his favourite chair like someone being forcing to sit on something spiky. To avoid noticing anything else she turned away completely, increasing the volume of the television. She snorted and laughed, but it had nothing to do with the fact that the character in the movie pulled the chair back just before his uncle sat down.

"Temi, we need to talk." He sat down on one bum.

She ignored him.

"Temi dear!" She frowned, but didn't turn or respond.

"Temi, Temi, for goodness sake, *Temi!*"

"Yes!" She hissed.

"I have been calling you. You want to act as if you didn't hear me. Please turn the volume down. We need to talk. "

"Mh-huh! Oya now!" she said, beckoning him to talk quickly.

"Please turn down the volume we need to talk." he said, pleading.

"Okay oh!" She pursed her lips, then pressed the mute button and subsequently turned to face him.

"I don't know how to say this...em..."

"That's a surprise!"

"Don't be mean nawh eh!"

"I'm not. You are acting like you're trying to make a business presentation."

"I have to travel to Scotland for a week."

"Okay, but I suspect something else. But it's okay, if you don't want to tell me. Mmh just make sure the other thing you wanted to say is not the type that can swallow a human head o! Okay, when are you travelling?"

"Tomorrow."

"Okay, safe journey." *You go tell me when you don ready, make God help you...*

"Thanks. I'll be off for squash in a few –"

"Do what you like, it's not like I can stop you anyway."

"There is something else."

"Say it already."

151

He considered it for a few seconds and said, "Never mind, some other time."

"If it is something that will carry or take my head, I better know now o! What is it?"

"Nothing really."

"Nothing eh?"

"Yes, nothing. I'm joining the boys for squash."

"Mh-huh nothing eh? Soon and very soon the cat will be out of the bag."

♥♥♥

Sigma, Osagie's cousin and Bassey his lawyer and friend from primary school, pelted Moses with the balls, he found it frustrating but it cured him of his other distractions. It was like they had a bad week and decided to pour it out in every shot fired. Moses only felt relief when they went on break.

"Why were you guys hitting the ball like that, you both seemed stressed out?"

"Oh really?" Sigma threw a towel around his neck.

"I saw Joanna." Moses sat down.

"Who's Joanna?" Sigma asked, twigging his racket.

"Bassey's ex."

"Na fine girl?" Osagie's cousin asked.

"I guess."

Osagie frowned, "What do you mean by 'I guess'?"

"Well she is..." He curved his arms around his stomach.

"What? Oh!" When he realised what his friend was doing, he added, "You act like it's a bad thing. You didn't bring your wife today, why?"

Moses shrugged.

"Your wife no longer comes to these sessions. She was like a glove that wouldn't just come off." Sigma retorted, nudging Moses

"You're talking about my wife." Moses replied, sounding annoyed.

"I really don't mean it in a bad way, was just trying to make a point."

"Point made, she's not. Case closed."

Ol'boy no be fight!" Sigma adjusted his shorts, "Listen!"

"You've been quiet my friend. What's the problem?" Moses slapped Bassey on the back.

Sigma shook his head at Moses.

Moses shrugged. When he received no response, he got up to stretch while asking Bassey, "Is your wife depriving you of what men look for in women or is it a bad week for business?"

"Is there an end to your banter?" Bassey spoke, quietly.

"What banter? I only asked a question." Moses hissed.

"You no see say the guy dey hungry?" Sigma asked laughing softly.

"See me see wahala o. You're a bit of an ogre, put it in there mate." Moses stretched out his hand to Sigma.

"Guys, just let me be." Bassey said in staccato.

"Wetin dey do this guy? Wetin hapun?" Moses whispered.

"You dey ask me? Ask am nah, no be your fault?" Osagie's cousin asked as he replaced his water bottle.

"Wetin I do? Bassey my guy wetin hapun?"

Everyone started laughing when Moses fell on the ground, nursing his jaw despite the fact that Bassey was nursing his hand.

"What was that for?" Moses appeared to be dazed.

"For causing me grief."

"Grief." he looking astounded.

"Two weeks bro, two fucking weeks!"

"What the hell are you talking about?" Moses now seemed agitated.

Bassey didn't hear him because he was already out of the court.

"Sigma, if you know something, say it, damn it!"

"Good grief, it's between you two." Sigma paused. "It's about his wife."

"Hhm, what has that got to do with me?"

"Your escapades are a big deal in our circle, i.e. the women of our circle."

"What?" Moses asked, obviously confused.

"Geez, are you suddenly daft? You've not been discreet about your mistress."

"What mistress?"

"Really? You wan form Jew for me? Guy na me be this o!" He turned abruptly to face Moses squarely. "Look, I see nothing wrong with having extra-marital affairs. Hell, I don't know, I've been doing it before you could imagine it, but I don't rub it in my wife's face. But you... everyone knows, and if your wife doesn't, then it's only a matter of time."

Moses looked away in shock.

"I remember the first time I saw both of you together I thought you just wanted to browse her website and log out. I didn't foresee marriage as a stunt you'd pull. Then you decide to nail it with another girl, not that it's a problem but you make her known to all?"

"Sigma, don't annoy me abeg!"

"Am I?

"So what's this about?"

"It's about you're sleeping with Olamide's PA." Bassey unscrewed his water bottle and sitting down simultaneously.

"We've already established that and I didn't know you were my watchdogs."

"No one says you shouldn't cast some lot out there, but isn't discretion something to be considered? Guy, you're not the first you know!" Bassey said quietly, assessing his racket.

"Is that why you punched me? Look at these guys oh! One woman, and you're all on my case. What of you wey dey change them like wrapper."

"We don't flaunt them," Sigma replied, stuffing his rackets into his sports bag.

"You don't flaunt them," Bassey corrected.

"How -"

"How we take know? We've got wives. You should be concerned because you marry white woman oh!" Bassey hissed, carrying his sports bag.

"Hey you guys!" Olamide strolled in, smiling.

They all looked at each other, shook their heads and then headed out.

Moses shook hands with Olamide, "You finally show up, after these men have panel-beaten me."

Sigma wore a mischievous smile and a slanted look. He opened his mouth then shut it.

"What is it?" Olamide asked.

"Oh nothing!" Sigma dropped his waste in the rubbish bin.

"I know you oh! Just spit am out quick, quick."

"Which levels nawh? Wetin be your own sef?" Sigma feigned annoyance as a guise to prevent further questioning.

Twenty

Athena took Wura shopping for things she needed to go back home with the following day – Athena's mother-in-law was in Austria for four days. She desperately needed Wura out of the way, seeing that she could no longer stand the competition, even though Wura was no longer sleeping with her husband. She wanted to ensure the distractions remained outside, increasing her chances of some intimacy with Moses.

For the time they'd been friends, Wura's stay gave Athena an excuse to fight for her marriage, but she had since lost interest in it. She had been pondering what Wura had mentioned earlier in the day: *something old, something new, something borrowed and something blue.*

She smiled absentmindedly at Wura who came out dangling three dresses across her body and did an Audrey Hepburn pose pouting her lips. *What does that mean? We all use it yet we don't have a clue of the significance.* She remembered she had to get them before her wedding: *my mother's pearl necklace, a blue garter, and Nadine's mother's pearl earrings and...I never got something new. Maybe I can salvage my marriage and making it my something new.*

Suddenly she felt confidence surge through her so while Wura tried on clothes she went to try clothes on too. She had already paid, and changed into some of them by the time Wura finished. She was going to her husband's office; she couldn't continue crossing and uncrossing her fingers. She needed to know how he felt about her and was willing to make any sacrifice necessary to make it work; and ultimately didn't want to end up like her mother.

♥♥♥

Moses' hand was inside Cindy's silk blouse, cupping one of her breasts when his wife walked in on them. He quickly pulled his hands out like a small child who accidentally touched a hot surface.

Athena whispered softly for fear she would betray her emotions. She hugged herself, and winced, not knowing what line of action to take; especially as a voice in her head advised her to scream, shout, and fight. Then it screamed at her to do something other than stand there, but she just remained there, motionless.

Moses tried to say something, but his voice faltered. Words weren't coming out; with slumped shoulders he lowered his head, and turned away.

Cindy stood defiant, rubbing her stomach, and moving her head like someone enjoying the feel of a cool breeze on a very hot summer day. She gave Athena a slanted look and a self-satisfied smile.

Athena couldn't take her eyes off her husband's occupied structure. He stared at nothing through the blind-covered window. She crumbled to the ground trying to grasp the floor as her head reeled. She managed to make her exit with unsteady legs. She took a taxi instead of her car, afraid that she would kill someone due to reckless driving.

Meanwhile Cindy saw it as the opportunity she had been waiting for. "Now...where were we? Let's get back to what we were doing before we were rudely interrupted." She purred and took her blouse off.

"I think it's time to call this off." Moses said, finally tearing his eyes away from the window.

"Call this off?" she asked innocently. She was pleased that it was Saturday, and there'd be no more interruptions. She had been longing for them to have sex in his office.

"This thing, whatever it is, is over."

"That will be difficult," she said, sounding stung.

"Why?"

"Because I'm pregnant!"

"Now? Suddenly –"

"That's why I came to see you today. Didn't I tell you that I had a surprise for you?" She sauntered over to his chair, and after fumbling with her bag, she produced an envelope. He frowned, then collected it. After reading it, he said, "Nothing has changed. I'm sorry, but I'm no longer interested. You can keep the baby if you like; I'll take care of it. But, that's all you'll get from me."

"Now you change your mind –"

"Please don't raise your voice."

"Or what? Don't raise my voice, don't raise my voice. Is that all you have to say after putting me in the family way?"

"Yes."

She laughed hysterically. "I'm sorry but that joke is for someone else, you told me you wanted me to get pregnant. I got off the pills, and now you expect me to do what?"

"I don't expect anything."

"Oh really? I'll make it easy since I have your mother's phone number."

"You wouldn't dare!" He walked closer to her, "If you do anything to further disrupt my marriage or hamper a resolution, you'll wish you were never even born."

Cindy shuddered and hissed. "You have no say in this matter o! I'm Nigerian, single and in love! Do you think I'm your wife that you can trample on and she'll say sorry? Your family already know about us so all I have to do is to tell them that I'm pregnant and I'll be your wife just like that." She clicked her fingers.

"Idle threats." He muttered, picked up his coat, before walking out. Seconds later, his assistant was at the door with keys in hand. Cindy stalked out, sulking. She stomped her feet like a child that has just been grounded by her parents.

♥♥♥

Olamide rushed in almost out of breath. He bent down to catch his breath. "Guy, I got it! I got it, man!" Olamide said, still breathing hard.

As soon as he regained his composure, he looked up to see Athena crouched, with tears in her eyes, but Olamide was on the opposite side of the room. They all seemed oblivious to his presence in the office, including the lady in the middle rubbing her stomach and wiggling triumphantly. The lady in question turned her head slightly, and he saw her dimple.

"What the fuck?" he swore under his breath. It felt like someone had hit him with a hammer when he realised who it was. She was smiling.

He walked out, closing the door. He punched the air, and jammed his hand on the wall, rubbing it to erase the pain. "Screwing two business partners? Friends! For fuck sake two best friends. Shit! Fuck, fuck, fuck!" Still furious, he laughed nervously for a while, and then picked up his phone.

He called the bank first. Then he called his driver. He called Cindy's landlord to cancel their tenancy agreement, but the man's number didn't go through; next he called the bank to cancel a direct debit he had set up for Cindy. She was due to receive her stipend the following day. When he finally spoke to the landlord they couldn't come to an agreement on cancelling.

Thinking of what to do, he remembered Dr. Ralph Barine who for three months had been bothering him. Dr. Ralph Barine was suspended due to his being investigated. Olamide didn't even know he had an appointment with the man at the time until he asked the secretary to book an appointment with the man.

Olamide tagged along while the landlord showed the man around, his mind going haywire. The boy with the tousled hair jumped off a girl he was on top of when the Landlord opened the door. Olamide asked him to leave. Dr. Ralph Barine, without hesitation, signed and collected a copy of the agreement then redeployed with his family two hours later. Cindy's things were stacked on the porch while the locks of the door were being changed, and the landlord watched the boy with the tousled hair pack the last of his things into a brown paper bag.

Twenty One

There were no more tears to shed, even though her eyes stung with them. She had been in bed for three days hiding behind a locked door; she wasn't even out of the outfit she bought on that day. She knew she couldn't continue living like this, but she didn't want to bring Nadine and Temitope into it. She heaved a deep sigh before going down stairs. She opened the fridge and remembered she hadn't done any shopping for weeks as a matter-of-fact. By the time she got back in the room, Moses was already there sitting on the edge of his side of the bed.

"Look Athena, it was a mistake."

"The fact that you were caught?" She hissed and dumped the apples on the dresser.

"I -"

"What did you see in her? No, what do you see in them? I don't want to hear what you have to say so this is what is going to happen. You will go up there, take your things, and leave. Do yourself a favour and tell your mother that she had better remain in Nigeria until you get a new house for yourself."

"Hon. I -"

"I have heard all I need to hear before now. The one that makes me cringe is that you had to sleep with the girl your mother brought under my roof. My bed!"

"I didn't, I swear!"

She sneered.

"Please, hear me out."

"You don't want to be a nuisance so don't forget to shut the door behind you." Athena said, walking into the bathroom.

He went towards it, but stopped when he heard the bolt.

♥♥♥

"Who can that be?" Moses' mother said when she realised it wasn't her alarm. "That useless wife of his should have been here; even to give my son a son is hard for her. All she knows how to do is to roam up and down with that mannerless girl. Maybe that Jamaican girl is tired of them if not why is she never with them." She grumbled.

She was still worrying about her aching body from a fourteen hours flight from Australia. She got up to go to harass the person at the door. "Yes, what can I do for you, eh?" Irritated to see a young lady.

"Ekasón Ma." Cindy kneeled.

"Eh!" she exclaimed. *This girl has manners. Something my daughter-in-law could learn.*

"My name is …is…" Cindy stammered, then started crying.

"What is it, my daughter?" She bent down near the door, not sure if it was right to let the girl in.

"It's Moses oh! Moses oh!" she replied, letting out another outburst.

"What did he do?"

"*Moti loyuñ o*," Cindy started crying again. "And now he wants me to have an abortion. I can't because my mother already noticed it before I did and has since kicked me out. It's God that saved me by sending my former classmate who is renovating her house and has allowed me to patch up there for the meantime."

"Wait o, my daughter, you say you are pregnant for Moses, for my son?"

"Sorry Ma, I didn't know you were his mother," she said, feigning shock.

"Who did you think I was?"

"I actually thought you were his sister."

"My daughter, come inside let us talk. Come, come, come." *So that boy really doesn't want me to have grandchildren, maybe the wife is not even the problem. Taah she is! If she was pestering him since he loves her, he would have succumbed.*

Cindy was with Moses' mother for hours looking for a polite way of escape from the smothering woman. She was saved by a message from Olamide, and asked to be excused.

♥♥♥

Olamide tapped Temitope till she woke-up. Squinting, she checked the time and got up immediately.

"What is it?" Temitope asked.

"I need to speak with you."

Temitope hissed, "At this time? Did you really have to wake me up at this time? Please save it till morning."

He nodded while she spoke willing her to immediately shut up and listen. But she pulled up the covers and lay down, simultaneously. He started tapping her again and each time she shoved his hand away.

"Why, why, why are trying to frustrate me of a good night sleep, eh! Olamide Ademinokan why?"

"I told you, I need to speak to you."

She sighed heavily. *This had better be good.* "Go on and say what you wish to say and make it quick."

"I don't know where to start."

"Then why did you wake me? Go straight to the point. I don't have all day... all night."

"I think I have impregnated someone." Olamide said, getting off of the bed. Temitope bolted upright, clear of all sleepiness.

"You think or you know?"

"A girl is pregnant for me."

"How far gone?"

"Four months."

"Four months? You were sleeping with another woman without condoms? Skin to skin? Is it that condoms became suddenly scarce? Did she get tested before you did that? God knows this life will be unbearable for you if I find out that I have any infection even if its thrush. I promise you hell..."

He fell silent again, not attempting to look up, knowing she was waiting to catch his gaze – strangely it was the only thing he remembered about her: her anger. He frowned, noticing that she was a bit calm, a bit too calm for the woman he had known for so long.

"Please tell me what to do."

"Un-impregnate her o, if there is any word like that."

"Are you suggesting an abortion?"

"I'm not suggesting anything o! Olamide, Olamide, Olamide I have suggested nothing. Now, can I sleep?" she lay down and for ten minutes she tossed and turned. "Thanks to you I can no longer sleep. Look here, Mister Man, let me make this clear: you are not marrying another woman. Ah! Unless I am not Temitope..." she laughed scornfully then scratched her head like a maniac and bit her index finger.

She threw off the covers, and padded downstairs to the kitchen. Her hands were shaking so much that when she poured herself a cup of coffee, the cup fell and shattered. When she bent down to gather it, a shard pierced her skin. She sat down and started crying.

She cried for a long time but she felt lighter.

For the first time in a long time her headache was gone, and she felt so relieved that she wondered why she never tried really crying more often. She could hear the crickets and knew it was morning; remembering her doctor's appointment, she made a mental note to cancel it as soon as it was 8am. She looked up to see Olamide tiptoe down the stairs with shoes in hand. She smiled and waited.

"Good morning," she said as soon as he alighted from the stairs. He jumped guiltily, dropping his suitcase in the process.

"Good morning. I didn't know you were awake."

"What would you like for breakfast?"

"I have to be off early..."

"What are you having for breakfast?" She asked, in a mock mean voice.

"Anything you could whip up quickly," he replied quickly.

He sat at the kitchen table, set the suitcase on the floor, then put on his shoes. He was moved to tears as he watched his wife prepare breakfast for him. *What was my excuse for goodness sake?*

Twenty Two

"Yes, what do you want? Haven't you done enough?" Cindy asked.

"I want the keys to the sedan."

"That one na water wey just pour for ground. Let me tell you how it's going to be: you are going to get me a place to stay, credit my account, and forget the car as these will be the least of your concern if your wife finds out."

Olamide sniggered. "She already knows."

"Does she know who with?" She asked giggling. "Maybe I should call her right now so we can settle this once and for all. What do you think?" She waved her phone.

Olamide's eyes widened. "All right, wait! Let's talk this over."

"There is nothing to talk about. My stipend is now four times higher. The clock is ticking."

He was aghast. Sweat glistened on his forehead, and his armpits started to itch.

"I'll do it after we've annulled our marriage, but not before."

"Na my head you wan use abi?"

"It's worth a try. I'll be back in an hour."

"If you get them within an hour, you get the annulment."

An hour later, she called to taunt him, which ended up aggravating him.

"You know what? Do your worst!"

"I see you're in a bad mood, 5pm then."

Each time an agent fell short, he thought of his wife – imagining how his wife was going to dissect him in various ways, and possibly throw his body parts across the country without leaving a trace. He felt like he had been curled and tied as he drove back to Cindy to negotiate with her to stay in a hotel or something until they found a place, even though he would prefer abandoning her where she was.

The predicament he now found himself in made him realise how much he loved his wife, and how difficult it was to think of a solution. He needed to think; he booked a hotel room, and told his wife that he was travelling. But first he needed to take out the 'fishbone' that was stuck in his throat.

He dashed home and told his wife that he had an emergency meeting. Then he made a mental note to inform Moses before the lie, like others, would collapse. Thinking of Moses made an idea spring up. *I can officially deny this. After all, she was with Moses. If only she signs these papers.* He couldn't trust Cindy to keep it away from his wife; he made up his mind to pay her to shift it to Moses. *Moses clearly was desperate, maybe not as desperate as his mother, but desperate all the same.* If Cindy agreed, he could reemploy her - as yet Temitope was not aware that he had sacked her. He would think of a good excuse to give his wife other than Cindy's incompetence.

He climbed the steps to the door, and wondered why the door of a house beside a major road would be left open. He shrugged, pushed the door further, then went in. He wanted to call her but he heard raised voices and inched closer. He didn't need to lean on the toilet door to overhear the conversation.

"Look, I'll not fall for that! Are you trying to trap me into marriage? I'm not ready to be a father, and that's that."

"Ty please, I didn't plan it."

"I don't care; you just have to get rid of it."

"But –"

"Look lady, I'm not going to be a father period. Besides, how sure can I be when you go snuggling other men?"

"I haven't, I promise."

"I saw you in a compromising situation with your boss –"

"Me?"

"Do bosses take their personal assistant's to private dinners or should I say candlelight dinners?"

"Let me –"

"At Zen Gardens? Is that its father?"

"I'm not cheating on you!"

"Just get rid of the pregnancy. We can't have a child out of wedlock."

"Believe me ..."

Olamide felt he had heard enough and tiptoed away. He climbed into his car. While he sat down drumming the steering wheel, the guy with brown tousled hair came out of the house.

"That must be the 'Ty,'" and his gaze followed the boy as he looked towards his right, then his left before crossing the road. The guy headed for the bus stop. Olamide turned the key in the ignition then turned it off when he saw Moses' number flash on his phone. They agreed to meet the following day.

♥♥♥

"Ol'boy yawa don gas o!" Moses pulled out a chair.

"I wan tell you say kasala don burst for my end sef!" Olamide sighed deeply with despair.

"Wetin hapun?"

Olamide recounted his story to his friend.

"I must first apologize for what I'm about to say," Moses took a sip of his beer. "I've been sleeping with your PA. On Saturday she met my mother while I and my wife went for this guy's stuff... You remember the guy who got chicken pox from stale meat Yeah? It was his twenty-fourth anniversary. Anyway, she told my mother that I asked her to get an abortion. It didn't matter that I told her to do what she liked.

Imagine your wife finding out from your mother. I've never seen Athena flare up like she did, and I've never known her to be so distraught that she has locked herself in her room for days. When she came out, she asked me to leave if I didn't take my mother with me. Or I'd have to choose between them."

Olamide hissed.

Moses looked at his friend with sympathy.

"What if they've given up on us?" Moses retorted, lost in thought.

"Wow! That's bad, really bad." Olamide muttered, his face suddenly filled with terror.

"She kicked you out? Now there's a first."

"Not that she threw me out but in her words, 'un-impregnate her'... The same girl who you claim is pregnant for you. Funny enough, I met someone else she may be pregnant for and his name is Ty. You know, I've seen you two together... the day your wife caught you."

Their phones rang simultaneously. Thirty minutes later they were shaking hands, and bumping shoulders with Sigma, Bassey, Osagie and Abraham. As they sat down Olamide looked up, nodding towards the entrance where Ty and a few of his friends were just arriving. Sigma questioned them until they recounted their whole event with Cindy.

Sigma got up, then was back a few minutes later with Ty. He pulled up a chair motioning Ty to sit down. After they'd exchanged pleasantries everyone fell silent, unsure of where to start. Then Sigma said, "Ty, you must know Olamide and Moses."

"I'm not sure... Olami is the boss."

"Olamide!" Olamide interjected.

"Well, Cindy is the common denominator, the reason we're all here. Em... technically." Osagie demonstrated.

"Sorry, I don't understand." Ty shook his head, confused.

"Cindy, the girl you're all shagging," Olamide said.

Bassey smacked the back of his head.

"What the hell? You call me here to tell me you're bashing my girlfriend? Who the fuck are you guys?" Ty asked, starting to get up.

Sigma was behind him, and pushed him back into the chair, holding him down with a firm grip. He bent down and whispered into Ty's ears. Then he lessened his grip, and eventually went back to his seat. Sigma looked at everyone before focussing his attention on Ty.

"We have a preposition for you: Cindy is fucking you, you and you but you are going to take the fall for an agreeable sum. You have to get a proof of paternity, what you call a DNA test." He nodded to Ty, who had now raised his hand.

"We had a fight, and I told her to abort it."

"How old are you?" Osagie asked.

"Twenty six years old."

Bassey's face looked grim, "Good, you're old enough to come up with something."

"Or don't you like money?" Osagie asked.

Ty hesitated and nodded slowly.

"How much is he charging?" Moses asked when he came back from the loo.

Everyone gave him a stern look.

Ty said, "Twenty thousand."

"Twenty thousand what?" Moses asked, horrified.

"Twenty thousand pounds." Ty repeated.

"Ole!" Olamide exclaimed, jumping up slightly.

"Oya, make una begin donate una money, five grand each."

Moses produced his wallet but came up with four thousand.

Olamide came up with three thousand.

Sigma collected it, and after summing it up, he gave Ty £5,000. He put the rest in his pocket.

"Ty, DNA test, and you'll get the remaining forty-five thousand."

"Forty-five thousand?" They all cchocd.

"Yes," Sigma looked at Moses and Olamide. "You asked me to handle it didn't you?"

"Okay." Ty said in a low voice. His head was fuzzy from the amount he heard. He got up quietly and left after collecting Sigma's phone number.

"Oya, Sigma give me back the remainder." Olamide opened his wallet as well as motion his friend.

"For why? You think say consultation na free? Come collect money make I see nah. I go show you as I take suffer get PhD. You dey craze o! Better pay for these drinks, let's get out of here. We are already beyond the limit. Who dey drive?"

"Wetin carry me enter this kin wahala sef?" Moses mourned.

"Na Oliver bin dey catch you sotey sotey your own no do you." Osagie said laughing.

"Say wetin? Na me you dey talk to?" Moses asked.

"No o! No be you, na the pesin wen dey your back I dey talk to."

Everyone laughed.

"But seriously guys, why? Why cheat on your spouses?" Bassey asked.

"I don't know oh!" Moses and Olamide chorused.

Olamide continued, "I've been doing this for a long time, and I recently got carried away." He paused. "You know the funny thing about all this? The simplest thing I used to know about my wife is all gone. Now I rack my brain to remember."

"Well, let's hope your wives are willing to take you back," Bassey said, ruefully.

"Good luck with that." Sigma grunted.

"Why?" Abraham asked.

"Welcome to our world!" Osagie said haughtily because Abraham had been on his phone since they arrived.

"Guys, which one una dey na, I never fit put mouth sef. Make una wait make man pikin marry first nah!" Abraham blinked, a little dazed.

"Before you started talking of your status, I wanted to say that Moses married a 'whitey' and God knows how many times Temitope has taken Ola Wizzy back. She just charged a little and he is shaking like a leaf. I just wished she had done it earlier." Bassey belched, and struck his chest.

Olamide's mouth fell opened, but he closed it, looking away.

"Are we staying all night?"

"Guys, I've got to go." Bassey stood up, stretching, "I go see una tomorrow."

"Woman wrapper!" His friends echoed, except Moses and Olamide, who were embroiled in their mind's utter perdition.

"I gree. At least I'll be in my wife's arms tonight!" He didn't bother to correct himself when they started to laugh.

♥♥♥

"Aunty, I need to speak to you urgently, are you at home?"

"Yes, is there a problem?"

"Not exactly Ma, but it's urgent."

In less than ten minutes, someone knocked on the door. Thinking it was a sales rep because her husband had travelled, she ignored it. When it continued, she roused herself.

She yanked the door open to find Cindy standing against one of the pillars on the porch with suitcases forming a semi-circle around her. Temitope frowned and shrugged it off almost immediately. When she saw the latest *Fendi* suitcases amongst the others, she stepped aside to let Cindy enter. Her frown deepened when she saw Cindy walking like someone carrying a gallon of water on her waist.

"What would you like to drink?"

"Water."

Temitope walked out and returned with it, stretched her hand. "Here."

"Thanks!" Cindy collected the plastic bottle and gulped its content.

Temitope continued to scrutinize Cindy's profile; her cheeks were puffy, her nose was now as large as her face. She wore clothes that were twice her size, and she looked rather unkempt. When she sat down it was as if she had a boil between her legs.

"Cindy!"

"Ma!" she responded, looking a little startled.

"Are you okay?"

"Yes Ma. It's just that I desperately need a place to stay for a few weeks, at least until I get a new place."

"New place? Why?" She was not sure she wanted to be a part of it.

"Yes, my landlord technically threw me out."

"Ha! I thought he was a white man and they didn't do that. What do you mean, 'technically'?"

"He is. He has a family member who just got into town."

"And he can't let you stay in the house? Were you owing him? As in, your rent, was it overdue? Did you do anything that is illegal to give him the audacity to do that to you?"

"None that I know of...." She looked down at her feet, "I'm presently looking for a smaller place to stay."

"That shouldn't be a problem, naturally. All you have to do is inform..." the phone rang. "Where have you been? You weren't even picking your calls at first. Athena, are you alright? Okay....Where are you...Okay when...that's okay I'll meet you there. No. He isn't around of course....I promise I'll be there on time."

"Aunty please, just for a few weeks and I promise I'll be out of your hair."

"You're staying here will not be a problem if my husband permits. You know that he's presently in Scotland." Temitope curled her feet up under her throw.

"Aunty, please..." Cindy dropped to her knees.

"You can stay here o! At least till my husband comes back..." she saw a mischievous smile across Cindy's face. "But you are restricted to the room downstairs. And you're to stay out of the kitchen. Don't worry I can take care of your breakfast, and sometimes dinner, but lunch should be easy since you work all day. The day you cross that line... well you just don't want to know."

"I...Eh..." Cindy stammered. "I'm no longer working."

"Say what?" Temitope almost shouted before turning to face Cindy squarely. *Them send you?*

"I was fired."

"Ha...Hmn...I'm not even going to ask why you were sacked, but you can't be in this house when I'm out, I'm sorry."

"No problem, Ma!"

"Good. The room is right that way."

Cindy walked towards the powder room, making a left to the room at the end of the hallway. She was carrying the last of the suitcases when...

"Are you pregnant? Is it for my husband?" Temitope asked.

Cindy stiffened, and didn't answer. She opened her mouth to answer when Temitope's phone rang again. Covering the mouth piece, Temitope said, "It's all right, ignore the question." As soon as the phone conversation was over, she sent her husband a text which read:

> *"If you like yourself, you'll cut your trip short and get back here. You have but three days before your grace period is over. THREE DAYS!"*

She loved sending such messages because it left him jumpy and out of sorts, wondering what she may have found out.

Olamide on the other hand decided to stay away for another three weeks when he found out that Cindy was now staying with Temitope.

Twenty Three

Cindy got prepared to meet Moses at *Jury's Inn* as they had agreed; she was so excited that she forgot the room number. She decided to call him after her meeting with Olamide. She didn't need to make up an excuse for Ty since she was going to be back before him. She hated lying to him, but he was all too nosy lately. To worsen it, their discussion hadn't gone beyond courtesy; he didn't even eat her cooking. He didn't seem glad to find out that he was the father, even though he demanded a DNA test like his life depended on it. She sighed as she stared at her shiny bloated face; she had run out of face powder. She applied just mascara and lip gloss; then tossed a piece of chewing gum into her mouth as she headed out.

When she got to the hotel, she had to wait in the lobby because he had stepped out. A few minutes later he called her up.

"What would you like to eat?"

"I'm not hungry. Let's just get on with the business at hand."

"Yes, that's true."

"This is where you will sign."

"You want me to sign before I set my eyes on the money?"

"Oh, sorry about that."

"Why are you so restless? Are you expecting anyone?"

"That will be none of your business."

"Well then... the money."

He showed her a cheque that he had already signed, she shook her head vigorously. Then he turned his laptop so that she could see the cursor was already on the confirmation button awaiting his pressing it. He was thinking of the excuse he was going to give to get the ball rolling.

"Well, you can now take whatever else you want, sex?" The words rolled out of her mouth before she gave it a thought. Ty hadn't touched her since he began to suspect her of being pregnant. She had been feeling so horny that she almost grabbed the postman. She read somewhere that it was a symptom for some women in her condition.

"Oh no!" he sprang back like something had just stung him.

"Why? Is it because I'm now showing?"

"Oh no, no, of course not, let's just order something to eat shall we?"

"Sure. I can eat and drink anything but I'm exempt from alcohol."

Olamide made a call.

Just then the alarm in her phone sounded. She sat up, surprised. "I have to be somewhere. I can't wait o!"

There was a knock on the door. She turned to face Olamide. "That was fast o!"

"I placed the order earlier."

"Oh! Can they give you take away?"

"I'll ask them."

He went to answer the door while she sank into the plush mocha-coloured chair. Moses and Ty came in. Moses walked towards her, wearing a smug smile. She was trying to adjust herself properly in order to get up. But when she saw what the 'room service' was, her feet buckled underneath her, and she plopped back into the chair. Moses with outstretched arms said, "Dinner is served." Not ready to face Ty she got up as quickly as she could and headed for the door.

By the time she had gotten to her new home, there was a parcel at the doorstep, too large for the letter box. She held it in one hand, and produced the key with the other. She tried the key several times, blaming it on her shaking hands. She finally opened the door, then slumped on the chair closest to her and kicked off her shoes without looking up until a woman shrieked, sending a man and a teenage girl running into the sitting room.

"What is it?" the man asked, a little agitated.

The woman pointed at Cindy.

"Who are you?" the man asked, his voice was a little shaky; he feared that it was one of his 'one-night stands'. He rubbed his hand vigorously against his thigh. His daughter folded her arms and watched her stepmother's hysterical display. Cindy glanced at them, one after the other, and was hit with a very bad feeling.

"Who is she?" the woman asked, without looking away from Cindy.

The teenager looked at her father, who was silently pleading with her. She stretched out an open palm, withdrawing it when her stepmother turned to the man, hands on his collar. He shook his head, and then raised his hand in surrender. He shook his leg, and the daughter dug his wallet out of his back pocket. Then she said reluctantly, "She is a lady I met earlier in the day. I can't give you the details."

"Why didn't you say anything before?" her stepmother blurted with contempt.

The girl shrugged and went to drag Cindy to the porch.

"My father doesn't want to see you, I believe that's obvious. Goodbye!"

"But –"

"Yes, he is married to that pathetic loser. But hey, you're no different! If you come back here, I'll call of the police." She laughed, scrutinised her father's wallet, emptied all monetary content and hopped back inside. The sound of the door slamming woke Cindy up from her daze.

He never rented this place! Olamide never rented this place. Unable to stand, she sat down on the steps, looked back at the house, and shook her head. *I should have made him press that button before he opened the door. How did they meet Ty? Oh, what have I done?*

She walked to the bus stop morosely; seeing a cash machine on her way, and decided to withdraw money, but there was nothing. Feeling sure that she didn't type in the proper information, she tried again, but got the same reply. She entered the bank to discover that every dime that she had saved over two years and all the money Moses and Olamide had ever given her was gone. "Ty!" she screamed before passing out.

♥♥♥

Temitope picked up her car keys, and drove for hours, hoping for the first time that she'd arrive at Bettina's house earlier than Athena. However, Athena was already there, sitting on the steps with blood-shot eyes.

"What is it?" Temitope asked, rushing to her friend's side, briefly forgetting her problems.

Athena shrugged her off. "Someone has beaten me to my husband's heart's desire."

Temitope looked from Athena to Bettina and back.

"Who?"

"Who do you think?"

"Wuraola? Wow, your mother-in-law will be glad." She said carelessly.

"She is in Austria."

"Where is the girl she came with?"

"At home."

"At home? Did you say 'at home'? Why didn't you simply kick her out?"

"Not here, in Nigeria."

"Oh!" she drawled.

"How did you know she was sleeping with my husband?" Athena asked, eyeing her friend suspiciously.

"Wasn't it obvious?" Temitope spat.

Athena wore a wry smile. "Yes, so obvious that I missed it, yeah? Why didn't I stop it then? I even cooked for him yesterday; they all ate my food, you know."

"You did cook? That's good." Bettina said.

Athena started crying again. "No it's not. They thought it was Wura that cooked it before she left. You know what, I'm tired. I can't take this anymore –"

"Take what anymore?" Temitope asked, confused.

"I'm going to get a divorce. God knows I'm filing those papers today."

"Are you sure?" Bettina almost shouted.

Temitope ran back to the toilet.

"Yes. I can't take any more of this from Moses. I'm tired!"

"You're letting your anger dictate your reasoning."

"No I'm not, I've been thinking of this for months. I've had enough!"

"Both of you need to get a grip. I'm too old to handle both of you the way you are going." Bettina leaned on the wall close to Athena.

"Going? I'm not divorcing my husband, not with two daughters... do you know what that would mean? He is a man. He will get married again, and the woman would probably give him a son. They would take everything that I've built and give it to her son. They'd leave nothing for my girls. No way! No, I'll rather stay and deal with him till all he will want is death. I'll make it to be far from him. Besides you can't cope with the hassles that come with divorce, plain and simple," Temitope said, firmly.

"It's obvious from your bickering that you still love your husbands. Have you considered the possibility of the girl's pregnancy being one of your husband's own? What will you do if it is?"

They fell silent.

"O God!" Athena exclaimed, with a sudden realisation of the implication of what Bettina said.

"God forbid, Ha –"

Bettina covered Temitope's mouth. "Shut up! Shut up if you don't have anything important to say. Ah-ah what is wrong with you?"

Athena broke down.

Temitope didn't understand how she was to feel; she couldn't sit comfortably on the step. She slid to the ground, tried to sit still and then started feeling an overwhelming urge to puke again. She pushed Bettina aside as soon as the door was open, and ran back to the toilet.

When Temitope got back they continued complaining, inciting, discouraging, encouraging, and grieving for each other before Bettina cleared her throat. When they didn't hear her, she raised her voice, "Shut up!" Still none of them heard her. They were exhausted and had not eaten for hours; they sat down on the step with their backs turned to each other, lost in their thoughts. "You're bickering over men you obviously love. Why don't you do something to salvage your marriage while you still can?"

Temitope scoffed.

Athena sniggered.

"Well, have you considered the possibility that the girl's pregnancy is for your husbands?"

"Ah! God forbid!" Temitope shrieked.

Athena laughed hysterically; she had been afraid of this because it would only show that she was the problem, but the doctor said she was all right. After everything she had done Moses still refused to get tested. Besides the girl was rubbing her stomach; what else would that mean if not showing off her pregnancy?

"You..." Bettina pointed at Athena, "you haven't given him a child yet, and if it's his, then society will believe that you're the one with the problem. And you..." pointing at Temitope, "You should know better, you think you can cope with playing cat and mouse in your home. If you can, for how long? Forever? Your home is supposed to be a haven, a sanctuary. Think again, you know the man you're married to. How long will it take him to find comfort in the arms of another woman?" Bettina said indignantly and added, "Sort yourselves out while I go and get ready."

"Ready for what?" Athena asked eagerly.

Bettina, stunned by Athena's keen interest, shrugged. "Well, I have to go to Queensbury," Bettina said, observing Athena.

"Where is Queensbury?" Athena asked, innocently.

"*Oyibo,* are you supposed to be asking that question?" Temitope asked laughing.

Bettina paused. "It's like when you fight with your siblings, you don't cut them off. No, you bribe them till you become friends again. You children of nowadays are so impatient that you don't realise that for a relationship to work, it requires hard work and tolerance."

Athena had lowered her head by this time; she may not have had a sibling – older or younger - but Nadine was relatively close to being one. When they rowed it was bitter, but none of them were able to keep malice, so about an hour later they would be bonding over a bucket of *Ben & Jerry's* and in the morning they'd gulp Andrew liver salts. She never got to find out if they ever took overdose.

Temitope blinked as she remembered when she had an argument with her second cousin, Tafiska; they settled it by fighting, with the agreement that whoever didn't win would do the other's chores for a whole week.

Tafiska and Temitope's sister Bimbo did keep malice with her on a regular basis, so much so that they'd draft their messages on papers. On one occasion she read all night in preparation for an exam she had in the morning of the following day. She had pleaded with her sister to wake her up. Bimbo didn't wake her up because she didn't apologize. She dropped a note instead. She woke up late, but when she got to school, she found out that the exam had been postponed.

"You're smiling. You seem to remember the good times..." Bettina smiled broadly, and clasping her hands. "Now you can use it to strengthen your resolve to make your marriages work."

Athena stared blankly before laughing.

Temitope laughed, scornfully. "I was thinking of a way to hack him into pieces and leave no evidence of it."

"I'm not supposed to be hearing these kinds of things from you." Bettina grumbled. "Where are your manners?"

"You've been watching too much crime drama." Athena responded, wearing an expression that was between frowning and smiling. She sat on the soft grass.

There was a short pause.

Temitope held her head, "I have a splitting headache."

"Alcohol?" Athena whispered.

Temitope nodded.

"I think I have aspirin in here...no, sorry, must have been in the other bag."

"What do you think?" Temitope asked, solemnly.

"About what?"

They were quiet for a while. Then Athena got up, and touched her backside. It was wet. She shook off her mac, spread it on the ground, then sat down again. Temitope watched Athena, but said nothing. She had already positioned herself down on the grass, with arms cradling her head, enjoying the warmth of the early morning sun. Besides, sitting down made her feel a little uneasy and queasy.

"You want to meet the girl?" Temitope asked.

"What girl?" Athena asked, a little irritated.

"Did I annoy you?"

"No, not at all!" Athena remarked, softly.

"You seem distracted, are you all right?"

"I don't know. You?"

"I don't know either! So... do you want to meet your husband's mistress?" Temitope asked in a whimsical tone.

"I don't know! What am I expected to do when I meet her? For one, I don't know how to get in touch with her."

"Leave that to me, but first, you have to join me in meeting my husband's mistress, because, if I go by myself, ha... something terrible may happen."

"What is her name?"

"I'm not sure. I know I have heard it before and seen her somewhere else. Why it escapes me, God knows..."

Athena frowned. She looked startled as a realisation crossed her mind. "You!" Athena said pointing, making a fist and walking around her friend. "It was you!"

"Me? What did I do?" Temitope looked at her friend amused, wondering what she was going on about.

"You brought that bitch to my house. Oh you!"

"Oh no, not you too!"

Athena eyed her friend, one arm akimbo and the other went through her hair.

"Cindy, that stupid girl! I brought that thing into my house..."

Athena gave a weird look.

184

"Forget my intention." Temitope paused. "Maybe that's how irony works."

Athena glared at her.

"I'm sorry I didn't think Moses... are you sure?"

"For fuck's sake, I saw her pants down in my husband's office." Athena smirked.

Temitope sat up, suddenly feeling dizzy, fell back. "She is pregnant for my husband."

"Yawn, yawn. We have to come to an amicable solution concerning this issue. We have to work something out. First we have to go to her house."

"That girl is not pregnant for my husband. Neither is she pregnant for yours." Temitope tried to sound convinced, while sipping water.

"How can you be sure?" Athena turned to look at her friend.

Temitope laughed nervously and vigorously shook her head. "It's not possible," she murmured, willing it to be a dream.

Athena felt she had had enough. She began to feel hot, thirsty, and very sweaty. She rubbed her neck, gasping for air, and peeling off her clothes. Her heartbeat increased steadily until she slumped.

Temitope saw her friend on the grass, and turned into a statue. She was dazed and wasn't calling for help. *What do I do? Em... what do I do now?* She started rubbing her arms to keep her warm even though it wasn't a windy summer day. When she finally summoned up strength she ran to the toilet to puke. When she came back, she just stared blankly, scratching her head.

Bettina came out and saw Athena lying still. She scrambled back inside to dial the emergency number. She forced Temitope to sit still. *I'm too old for this!* While they waited for the ambulance to arrive, Bettina sprinkled water over Athena. Temitope stared at her friend. Her stomach rumbled making her feel like something was being cooked inside it.

Six minutes later, the ambulance sped through traffic. Bettina followed Athena in the ambulance while Temitope followed, driven in her car by Clinton.

"I got you, you're all right." The nurse said when Athena stirred.

As soon as they got to the hospital, Temitope ran into the toilet; she didn't realise it was the wrong she had entered until she saw urinals. She made a few call; after advising her husband to call his friend, and Nadine, she decided to be tested. She needed to find out what was wrong with her since the pills for the stomach bug were not working.

♥♥♥

Temitope was beginning to feel nauseous from the smell of medicine when the doctor came towards them. Bettina met him half way.

"She is stable for now." The doctor said.

"Can we see her now?" Bettina and Nadine asked, almost shouting.

"She is on a sedative right now but you can go in."

"Thank you so much." Bettina patted the doctor's hand.

"It's all right, it's my job," The doctor said.

"I feel..." Temitope slumped just in time for the doctor to catch her, and call for assistance.

Twenty Four

Moses had been calling Athena's number, but she didn't pick it. Since she was weak, she didn't want to concern herself with him. She tried to sit up. Bettina tried to push her back but she brushed Bettina's hands away. He had left a message:

> *"I'm sorry Athena! I let a mistake get out of hand. I'm sorry. Please forgive me."*

The machine started to beep, and her friend was carted away. An hour later, the doctor came out of the room, and asked for Bettina, Nadine, and Temitope to join their friend.

Bettina looked at the doctor suspiciously, and something occurred to her. She peered into Athena eyes, then into the hollow part of the neck between the collarbones, then opened her palm. She proceeded to do the same with Temitope. She raised her hands up, and started dancing and singing. Athena and Temitope waited for her to finish before asking her, "What is it?"

"You're both pregnant."

"Amen o! It shall come to pass o!" Temitope said.

Athena amused, just stared at Bettina.

The doctor walked in to congratulate them, and discussed the hospital's antenatal provisions.

"I knew I was fertile, but I needed to be sure....oh my God!" Athena covered her mouth as tears welled in her eyes.

They hugged each other, and sobbed until they were relieved.

"He cannot know about this. Please don't tell!" Athena pleaded like her life depended on it.

"Why not? This is good news," Nadine retorted.

"Please! I need to know that he loves me for me."

"Does it matter?" Bettina asked.

"To me it does. I need to find out if I will need to get a divorce."

Nadine shrugged.

Bettina frowned and sighed.

Temitope was in her own world, feeling nauseous as the smell of penicillin wafted in and end up expelling her stomach's content in the silver bowl a nurse was holding.

Bettina's phone rang; she stepped out, and came back a few minutes later. "My daughter, Cynthia is back. Clinton is bringing her here."

"No way!" Athena responded excitedly. "Are you all right?"

"Yes, I guess I'm nervous. Is that normal?" Bettina asked.

They all laughed.

"There is nothing normal about you, Bettina," Athena said.

"Well, we finally get to meet our generation's version of Bettina. Not that you are old or anything." Temitope said and Nadine and Athena poked her.

Thirty minutes later, Clinton came in.

"Where is she? She is supposed to be with you." Temitope asked him.

"Take it easy, she went to ease herself. Let me go in search of her."

Cindy walked in.

"Cindy!" Temitope and Athena exclaimed.

Temitope dropped the cup in her hands.

"No, Cynthia!" Bettina beamed excitedly. "Cynthia, I want you to meet my... they're more or less my children too. Athena, Temitope and Nadine, I want you to meet my dear daughter," she added, oblivious to the change in the atmosphere.

The whole room had gone as quiet as the graveyard; it was like a cold wind had come in because Athena and Temitope's countenance had changed; Even Cindy's had changed, although hers was of shame and embarrassment. Bettina was more confused than Nadine. Nadine gave Bettina water, and she gulped quickly and then started coughing. Luckily, Temitope was there in time to start rubbing her back until it stopped. Athena pointed at the girl who she had caught with her husband.

"Oh, I went to look for you. What did I miss?" Clinton looked at everyone. "Ah, I see! You're the thorn." Cindy brushed past him as she made her exit, then she ran to the chapel. Unable to sit down comfortably she curled up in a ball at one corner, crying. She finally realized who the women in her mother's life were. Sadly, they were the women that saved her only brother's life, and gave her mother a complete family. She felt like she did before she ran away; an alien.

♥♥♥

As soon as Bettina went home the following day, Temitope huddled closer to Athena, speaking in a low tone.

"Pardon?"

"Let's give them a run for their money."

"I don't know what you mean?"

"Let's call our husbands' bluff."

"How?"

"Let's tell them that we want a divorce."

Nadine came in with three steaming cups of coffee, glad that she wouldn't have to share. "What if they want it and have been waiting for you to bring it up?"

"That's a good idea. I'll get to know how Moses really feels about me. Oh, this smells nice."

"Are we allowed to drink coffee in this condition?"

"Don't know." Athena cleared her throat, "Besides pregnancy is not a disease."

"Look who is talking. What I got when I was pregnant was little compared to what I'm going through for this one. I'll make him sweat." Temitope smiled dreamily.

"What if it is another set of girls?" Athena asked.

"What is that thing about the XY chromo-something?"

"The XY –"

Athena touched Nadine's hand softly. "It was more like a rhetorical question, dear."

"Oh!" Nadine sounded disappointed.

"Nadine sweetheart, we will need your husband's help for this." Temitope smiled sweetly.

"My help for what? Hello ladies? The loves of my life." Nadine's husband looked at them curiously after kissing his wife.

Temitope told them of her plan, and they weighed options. Nadine's husband suggested what they could do to prevent hitting their husbands below the belt, but something that would be close enough. Athena and Nadine made more changes to the plan so that by 11pm that night, the plan was flawless; it was to swing into action the morning of the following day. The women agreed to assist Nadine whenever they were not throwing up - which Temitope almost always did or pretended to do sometimes.

Nadine's husband was glad to put his paternity leave to the test, especially since their baby was teething early, and gave them restless nights. He looked at his wife adoringly, and whispered, "Remind me never to cheat on you."

♥♥♥

Bettina took Athena, Temitope, and Nadine with her to church for Thanksgiving a few months later; her daughter wore a tight dress and stomach was rotund to almost breaking free from the dress.

A week before, Cindy apologized to them when they came to meet her – she never went back home after leaving the hospital. Athena and Temitope were secretly overjoyed that their husbands were not responsible for the pregnancy. They were both willing to support Cindy transition to motherhood and even after and were especially willing after Nadine and Athena found out that Ty was actually Desmond Stone.

Epilogue

Athena looked dreamily at her babies. She held her second baby in her arms, rubbing its nose as Wura's words echoed in her head, *'something old, something new, something borrowed and something blue.'* As if to jinx it Wura said, "This time, it really is something new." The birth of a new baby was usually a time for reconciliation. That's why Athena allowed her mother-in-law carry each grandchild in turn.

Moses bent down, and kissed her, snuggling closer. He thanked her. He adjusted his weight then brought out a parcel. She exclaimed when she saw what was inside; it was a replica of a necklace she had misplaced since before they had been married.

"How?" Athena asked.

Moses touched his nose lightly, saying nothing.

A few minutes later, a baby was crying then another. Everyone looked at each other and shouted, "TWINS!" They were still cleaning Temitope up, when she threw the curtain that separated them open. She shouted at them to bring Athena's baby for her to see. She insisted that the nurses bring her babies beside her, then looked at her husband, who was smiling gleefully, like someone who had been given a new set of teeth. "Will you close your mouth already?"

"But –" Olamide started to demonstrate.

"You have the boys you wanted so get on with it. Don't come to my bed again, you hear me? Phew, I didn't know boys could be such hard work."

Bettina laughed. "They always say that!"

When Temitope found out that Athena had twins, she shrieked excitedly, startling all of the babies in the room. "I didn't know twins ran in your family!"

"Neither did I!" Athena responded, alarmed and smiling.

"Okay, make we begin waka!" Temitope said, almost shouting.

Wura tried to slide a finger into the hand of one of Athena's babies. "Waka go where? We're snowed in."

"Snowed wetin? In a hospital?" she exclaimed.

One of her sons started to howl. She turned to him. "My dear, get used to this, because you'll be hearing more of this.

Everyone laughed.

Thank you for reading my book. Please leave a review of what you thought of my book at your favourite retailer.

Like me on Facebook: http://facebook.com/kemka.ezinwo

Discover other title(s) by Kemka Ezinwo
Twerking Cruxes and a Cloaked Visage